THE DEVIL'S GARDEN

Written by Written Out Loud Crew 189

Ben Sleeper
Hudson Schunk
Maté Blier
Olivia Romain
Veronica Paré

Under the direction of Josh Shelov
and Written Out Loud Studios

Cover design by Naomi Giddings

ISBN 978-1-387-69103-6

This book is dedicated to all the loving parents and supporters of this crew, and to each other.

CONTENTS

"The devil's finest trick is to persuade you that he does not exist."

– Charles Baudelaire

PROLOGUE

The boy watched from the inside of the bureau as the Devil ascended the staircase. He was a tall, thin man, lithe and sinewy, his pale hair, receding at the temples, combed neatly back. He moved with a catlike, unnatural grace, trailing one milky, long-fingered hand along the polished oak banister, its nails cut into perfect, unpainted ovals. He appeared to be around forty in age in his slim ash-colored suit, though this was simply his preferred form.

He was clean-shaven, with an aquiline, beaked nose and wide-spaced eyes. As he caught sight of the boy, his full, red lips curved into a smile. The Boy knew that smile. It promised pain. It spoke of retribution, and if the boy knew his father, whatever the Devil had planned was going to be very, very slow.

Even in the darkness of the early dawn, the Devil's eyes shone, like stars smoldering, burning, yearning to escape their prisons of cold, hard ice. His tall, polished black boots of an unknown leather reflected the pearly, white orb of the full moon, visible through the high, arched gothic window behind him, in their shiny, mirror-like surface. He paused on the landing, and licked his lips in anticipation. Tonight's first act had been a failure, but a long anticipated second, a fallback of sorts, awaited him past the next six steps.

Within the cabinet, the boy shivered. The aura coming off of the "man" mere meters away was unlike anything he had felt anywhere else, so alien yet so bizarrely familiar, a feeling of being simultaneously lonely and not alone at all, each an equally disturbing prospect.

The man conjured a snowy white handkerchief from within his sleeve and pressed it to his forehead, frowning slightly as he withdrew it, soaked with viscous golden ichor.

It bothered him. That woman was one of the few living things who could make The Devil bleed, a reminder of his own vulnerability, however infinitesimal.

No matter. She is gone now. No one would ever harm him again, least of all the cowering, pathetic boy, trying to use the darkness to hide him. The fool. The man was the darkness, and had been born into it. He was as fathomless, as untouchable, as inescapable as the star-flecked sky outside. The dark was his home, and he could not be beaten at his own game.

"Come out, come out, wherever you are," He beckoned, playfully.

The Devil climbed the last few steps, and stopped directly in front of the bureau, as though lost in thought. With a fluid, sudden movement, he reached down, through the crack in the doors, and lifted the boy to his feet. The child tried to cry out, but no sound emerged. It mattered little. No one would be awake at this hour, and eerie noises were known to emanate from the old Primogeni House, abandoned since the early eighteenth century. The locals called it Mansion Diable for a reason. If only they knew just how accurate the name truly was.

"Tut-tut. You have been a *very* naughty boy, my dear Preston," He chided, as the boy desperately tried to flee, to escape the horror and never think of it again forevermore, held in a state of suspended animation by the Devil's power, his face a frozen image of pure terror, like a death mask.

"Elizabeth?" The man called.

From the shadows stepped a girl, not much older than Preston, gray-eyed and grim-faced. A small sheath sat at her hip. She stared, wide-eyed, and the struggling boy stared back.

"Fetch me the rings, darling."

The girl darted off. When she returned, she was holding a small box covered in smooth, black velvet.

The Devil took the box from her and flipped it open. From within, he retrieved two shining, thin wedding bands of radiant gold. He held one of them in the palm of a spidery white hand, gazing at it in contemplation for a moment before turning back to Preston.

"You know, I wore this very ring myself, years ago, at my wedding. Now I will pass it on to you."

He deftly slid the band over the second finger of the boy's left hand.

Almost instantly, it began to shrink, getting smaller and smaller until it disappeared into his pale skin, leaving only a small cut behind. As beads of blood dripped down onto the floor, The Boy's eyes screamed silently.

"And yours, Elizabeth."

With a sense of great trepidation, the girl held out her hand.

As the second ring shrank into oblivion, the Devil gently took Elizabeth's hand, and pressed it against the unresisting hand of the frozen boy.

Two crimson droplets of blood slid down from where metal had cut into flesh. The Devil placed a small glass vial beneath, and the drops downward and mingled within. Capping the vial, he slid a supple silver chain through a small loop in the top, placing it around his own long neck. Giving it a pat, he smiled oddly.

"I'll keep this safe for now."

He turned to leave, and then seemed to remember something that he had omitted to mention.

"Oh, and, Preston? I forgot to say. As repayment for your actions, I have a gift for you, however little you deserve it."

He bent down, and whispered into the boy's ear.

"For as long as you live, you will love. But will scarcely find it before tragedy strikes its moral blow."

The Devil straightened.

"Come, Elizabeth."

As the heavy door swung shut behind them to the sound of the Devil's cold, clear laughter, the boy crumpled, immobile no longer. As the delayed scream escaped his lips, he struggled to his feet and, grabbing his mother's ragged coat off of the rack and pulling it around him, ran like a startled, wounded beast, across the hall and onto the porch before collapsing, falling prone in a shivering, weeping heap as snow gently drifted down.

CHAPTER 1

The Opening was my only place of comfort at this Coventry Garden School. It was the only place that made me feel at peace. The Opening was a clearing in which the thick forest trees of the Scottish Highlands parted, and the sun shone down nourishing all of its creatures; flowers and animals alike. I was walking there now, stepping over the hundreds of shallow stumps that the founders of the school needed to build Coventry Garden. After a bit of annoying stumps, were the Vines. The Opening's natural defense mechanism. Anyone daring to come through the vines (other than me of course), was embarking on a very spiky journey. They were spines emerging from the trees, sharp and ragged, and there was only a small passage to get through the labyrinth of spikes. I walked along the vines carefully dodging the blades that protected The Opening. I was only 100 feet away from The Opening's beautiful embrace of light when something caught my attention. It was a glove. Sky blue, and silky, and soft. It was Elizabeth Grey's. My secret love, and my reason for going to this drab school. Elizabeth Gray was the most beautiful angelic creature that God ever could have created. I picked up the glove gingerly, careful not to tear it (or my flesh), and stuffed it in my pocket.

"*When Monday comes around, I can give it to her and then maybe she will give me a decent amount of attention.*" I squeezed through the last few feet of the Vine, and I was practically in The Opening when I saw her. She was watching the birds play, and feeding the squirrels pieces of her Singing Hinny. She was smiling, her white teeth shining in the sun, and her baby blue dress was perfect with the lush environment. I was standing there, watching Elizabth Grey's heavenly features for who knows how long, until my fantasizing of her was drowned out by heavy footsteps.

"Ow, ow! These blasted spikes! I'm getting cuts all over the place!"

Someone was coming towards me. I quickly moved out of the way to hide, and perfect timing too, because right as I did Darcy Jones came strutting out of the Vines. Darcy spotted Elizabeth and immediately forgot about the spikes that were spearing his flesh.

"Liz... You look absolutely stunning. How did you manage to get all through here without tearing your clothes? I sure didn't succeed," he said embarrassed, as he looked down at his torn, dirty clothes.

"Luck, I suppose. And don't worry Darcy you look absolutely fine. Come sit with me. I have one more Singing Hinny, and we could split it," Elizabeth's angel voice said sweetly.

She scooted over from the bench and patted the space next to her. Darcy happily took the invite and sat next to her. It was then that he realized the true beauty of The Opening. He smiled, and took half of the Singing Hinny out of Elizabeth's offering hands.

"Liz, why is it that you have Singing Hinnies? I mean, I thought Headmaster Greengrass said we weren't allowed to bring them outside of school groun-"

"Since when have you ever cared about what Headmaster Greengrass says?" Elizabeth giggled. Darcy flushed a shade of red, and he should have. He never ever followed the rules, and was constantly at the Headmaster's office.

" I just... I want to make sure that you don't get in trouble," Darcy replied. He looked at the ground embarrassed.

"It's alright silly. Besides, do you forget my father is the most famous shipman in the country? The Headmaster wouldn't even dare look at him if he had the option," she replied.

She giggled and took a bite of the Hinny.

"You know that boy, Preston?" Darcy asked.

Immediately, I gasped. They were talking about me. Elizabeth nodded her head (a relief because I didn't even know that she knew I existed).

"His father works for mine. They are not the best of friends. I wouldn't be surprised if they didn't know we both go to Coventry Gardens. Oh! I almost forgot Darcy, I lost my glove in the spikes, did you see it?" She changed the subject, and my heart fell.

Maybe her father had told her horrible things about our family, and she was ashamed to talk about me. My father tried hard, but still wasn't the best of workers. Luckily, Darcy followed along with Elizabeth's annoyance.

"No. Nothing caught my eye. I must admit I wasn't particularly looking for it though," Darcy answered ashamed.

He looked down at his feet and started playing with the grass. Elizabeth smiled, but underneath it, I could tell she was annoyed.

"It is quite alright. Well on that note, I would like some alone time so if you would please leave that would be greatly appreciated," Elizabeth said like sour, spoiled honey.

Darcy quickly got up and practically ran away. It was clear that when Elizabeth was annoyed, she was not the person you wanted to be with. But I had promised myself so many times that if I ever met her, I would not annoy her in the slightest bit. She soon got over Darcy and was back to feeding the animals and watching the birds. The sun shone down on her like a halo, and my dreams went back into action. I loved Elizabeth, and when I returned her glove tomorrow, maybe, just maybe she would love me back.

CHAPTER 2

I looked at the silver watch on my wrist, then at Darcy, " I have to go" I said, interrupting him. He blinked his shiny hazel orbs a couple of times with a confused look lingering on his face.

" I thought we were going to the park?" he spoke in his clear voice.

I looked him in the eyes and put on my best-acting face.

"Yes, I know, but I remembered I have some schoolwork to finish," I said as an excuse, as quickly and believable as I could.

"But we have all our classes together," he pointed out to me.

I said the first thing that came to mind.

" I was recommended by our school counselor to switch from history to geography in the third

period," I said, convincing myself along with him. "I suppose I'll be switching classes now. And the teacher for geography gave me all these notes, telling me to go over them so I'm not completely lost," I said.

Darcy lightened up for a second, then went confused again.

"But history and geography are practically the same things, no?"

I shook my head.

"Oh no, very different things," I said.

I crossed one of my arms under my chest and put the other one on it, resting my head on my fist. "But I should get to that, have a great evening," I replied.

I turned on my heels and started walking away, hurrying more and more with every step.

I opened the drawer in front of me and took out a pair of elbow-length black gloves. I placed them on my bathroom counter as I looked at myself in the mirror. My green eyes were slightly red and unnaturally lit, it was wrong. I pushed it aside, this was something I *had* to do. It was an order. I grabbed a small silver dagger, it was about the size of my hand, and threw it into my bag. I added a spare change of clothes to it as I walked into my kitchen.

I lived alone in an apartment, but I told people that I had parents who were rarely home, and when they were they fought often, just so they wouldn't dare come over. I put my bag on the table as I sat down with a piece of paper and a pen. I carefully forged his penmanship as I wrote.

To whoever finds this,

I'd like to start by saying that there was nothing you could have done. I would have died someday, I just chose to do it earlier than expected. And I know that you're thinking of why I did it. I truly had no choice, it was like the whole world was against me. People who couldn't keep their own opinions to themselves and took pride in hurting others. And I don't want to be here to see the world get destroyed by that.

The only person that actually made me smile was the person to whom I could relate too. She also had parents that were always gone. And when mine did come back, they were always more excited to see her. So thanks, mom and dad. And to everyone, you get to know that you are the cause of this. And that nobody knew how I felt, I gave myself less acting credit than I deserve. But when word gets out of this, which it will, they will all start acting like they were my best buddies. Because that's what people are like. They ignore you until they come into the picture. Until they are asked about you. Then they convince everyone that they tried to talk you out of it, that they tried to help you. But when in reality, they caused it. So once again, thank you for that.

In hopes that the people of this cruel world meet their deserved fate,

John D.

I looked over it and I was satisfied. It was something he would write. How did I know? I was his friend. Got too attached you could say. Despite being told not to. I wouldn't make that mistake again. I grabbed my phone and dialed his number. He picked up on the third ring.

"Hello?"

"Hey, John, are you busy?" I asked him.

"Hey, Liz! Nope, I'm free at the moment, why?"

" I was wondering if I could come over for the night. My umm, parents are fighting." I turned on my recording of two people fighting with each other just loud enough for him to be able to hear it faintly, but not loud enough to hear the exact words.

"Oh Liz, of course, it sounds pretty bad. You can come now," he assured me, the sound of sincerity and sympathy was easy to hear. I sighed.

"Thanks, Johnny," I said and I hung up.

Step one is complete. I put my coat on and my boots as I walked out of my plain apartment and locked the door behind me. Down the hallway of the first floor, and outside.

My apartment was in the center of my little town, my school a ten-minute walk on the other end of town. My boots clicked as I walked down the cobblestone streets. The crisp and cool breeze made my cheeks go red. And the evening had started to set. I gripped my bag tighter to my chest as I walked faster, desperate to get this out of the way. The sooner the better. I walked up to his house and looked around making sure that nobody saw me as I knocked on the dark green entrance door. His chocolate eyes lit up when he opened the door, and his dark hair was a tangled mess on his head.

"Are you okay Lizzie?" I nodded.

"Are your parents here?" I asked him. He shook his head.

"No sorry, I know they really like you but they had to go to a friend's marriage. But it's okay if they come home early I'm sure they will be thrilled to see you, they definitely will be more than me," I smiled a sad smile.

Then he leads me to the spare bedroom. To the room with gray walls, a small dresser with a dirty mirror above it. I walked over to the small single bed with a pink quilt on it. I have slept here countless times. I put my bag on the ground and fell onto it making the comforter fold a bit and the frame squeaked under my weight. I closed my eyes but opened them when I heard John come up to the door.

"Thanks again," I told him.

"It's no problem," he assured me. I got up and hugged him for the last time. "Come I've got your favorite movie ready."

He left and ran downstairs and I choked down a sob, he didn't deserve this. But it had to be done. Or else it would be the end of me.

People *are* selfish.

I walked behind him and then sat down in the armchair beside him. He was sitting on the ground, against the couch. I still didn't understand why he never actually sat on the sofa.

* * *

Hours later he was asleep. And I slowly crept out of the gray-walled bedroom with my dagger in my gloved hand. His bedroom door made no sound as I opened it. I walked past the blue walls that were littered with photos and awards to get to his bed. I slowly lifted the covers off of him. "I'm so sorry, I wish I didn't have to do this to *you*." I raised the dagger up and then brought it down into his stomach, twisting it to the right. His eyes snapped open and I put my hand over his mouth. He made no loud sound, but the ones that did escape sounded utterly heart-breaking. His red blood started leaking out of his mangled stomach and as I delicately put a couple of fingers to his neck, I barely felt a pulse. Tears left my eyes and it was the first time that had happened. It was definitely because I got attached. Why couldn't I have just taken the Devil's advice? As the boy under me finally stopped breathing, I took my hands off the dagger and left it there. I left the note I'd forged on his bedside table and left John's eyes open. It seemed more natural. I quickly got my stuff and left his home, once again making sure nobody saw me.

* * *

I rushed into my apartment and got into the shower. I had a bit of his blood on me and I wanted it off. The warm water surrounded me quickly and it helped relax me a bit. I scrubbed my skin raw once again and thoroughly cleaned my hair. I got out and changed into my pajamas. Throwing my blood-soaked shirt into the stainless-steel sink I owned along with some soap, I kept adding more and more of the cleaning liquid until the whole sink was a large bubble and the shirt was perfectly white once again.

I walked into my room and up to the large painting on my wall. I carefully pulled the painting of a lady out of the frame, revealing a board with red pins and red ribbons on it. Small pictures of people were what the pins and ribbons decorated. Marking the process on a piece of paper in red ink, I proceeded to look over my board.

It'd been a while since I updated it. I disposed of the pictures of past victims and looked upon the few that were still on the board. I traced John's photograph before I threw it in the trash, tears and regret filled me. It was a photo of him on picture day at school. Thinking over all the murders I'd done in my life, this was the first time I regretted killing someone. And it was all because I GOT ATTACHED. I got attached to the boy's warm smile and terrible jokes. His ability to remember every detail and the kindness he gave to those who didn't deserve it, to me. Damn, I hate it when that wretched Devil is right, I'm going to bed.

CHAPTER 3

I have had a feeling that Rent Warmth was my father's right hand man for as long as I could remember. Ever since I could first understand English, my father had tried to make me his evil sidekick, his heir. But I had always refused to be evil, and my father hated me for it. So when I was 4, my father recruited a fellow 4-year-old to train to be his heir instead. He had hoped using someone my age would make me jealous, and hence bring me over to the dark side. Instead, I could care less. But it has always intrigued me who it might be, for he said I knew them.

And so Rent was the first to come to mind.

Rent Warmth has bullied me ever since I first met him. On the first day of school, he tried to wrestle me but I said my mother would never have allowed me to wrestle. He never stopped making fun of me for my pacifistic views. He would push and shove me in the hall all the time. The teachers never cared too much if they witnessed it, and Rent warned me what would happen if I ever went to a teacher. So I let it stay how it was.

Even though Rent was bad to me, he never seemed to be much of a bother to anyone else. He never even bothered my best friend Coley. Usually when he comes up to me to pick a fight, if Coley is with me, he will be respectful. "How do you do, Coleton?" Phony.

As we have aged, his bullying and fighting have become more of a tradition than actually fighting. I even managed to make a deal with him that we can only 'fight' (which is him wrestling and me dodging), on Tuesdays and Thursdays from 3:20 to 4. Shockingly enough, he has managed to oblige to our compromise quite well.

Rent even bought me a watch for my birthday 3 years ago. I don't understand Rent.

But on the topic of that watch, I am thankful for it. Over the past few years, I have found old watches in the trash and refurbished them to top shape. I have accumulated 18 watches over the years, and only 5 of them were bought new (4 of them from Coley and that one aforementioned one from Rent). I like to keep to a specific schedule, week in and week out, so I have all my watches set for different days. I have my 7 best watches set for each day of the week, and my other 11 are only used on days where I will have a change in schedule.

Most people in the school think I am weird for having 18 watches, each set for specific things, but I don't understand how they can be so unorganized with their time. Most people at school will change their plans easily, but I find it hard to do. Rhythm and repetition help keep me going. Organization is key.

Coley is one of the few people who understand me. I have turned him into a repetition guy as well. Coley has been loved by everyone in the school ever since he came here in 3rd grade. The teachers adore him for his manners and smarts.

Even though The Coventry Garden School is technically a boarding school, most people's families live in Scotland. But Coley was born and raised in Amsterdam. He came here because of his twin brother Quintin, who was a troublemaker back at home. I don't mind Quintin, but we normally stay out of each other's way. Coley and Quintin are *apparently* identical twins, but there is nothing identical about them. Quintin is 3 inches taller than Coley, he has darker hair, and he has a bent nose, one which he sustained while falling down a flight of stairs some years ago. They have completely opposite personalities as well. Coley is one of the nicest people you will meet, and while quiet, he gets along with everyone. Quintin, while Coley says he's not a bad student, would much rather be doing anything else that isn't academic, and he talks *a ton.*

In 5th grade, I don't know how, but Coley convinced me to take Latin in 6th grade. Somehow I ignored the fact that the Latin teacher was the most feared teacher in the whole school, and possibly all of Scotland. Everyone in the whole school was scared of the 43-year veteran, 71-year-old Mr. Emerson Frond.

Latin ended up being the first period class.

21 brave souls entered Mr. Frond's classroom that September morning. That was the most incoming 6th graders to take Latin in the past 3 decades. Byron Franks

told everyone that his cousin said for us all to sit in alphabetical order in order to not get scolded. Byron Franks was the largest teacher's pet in the grade, and while normally that was a bad thing, in this case we all thought it could save us a lecture. For the entire time before the bell, he herded everyone into their order, and as the bell rang, we all walked single file into the room.

Mr. Frond was not there, but we all sat very still. Every notebook was on a desk, everyone sat straight up, eyes towards the center of the room, everyone's hands folded together on the center of the desk. No one dared make a sound with the threat of Mr. Frond entering the classroom at any moment. 7 minutes passed, with still no sign of Mr. Frond, yet no one moved. The loudest noise was my watch ticking.

I had to go to the bathroom really badly, so I was planning on silently getting up until Phoebe Hills started whispering.

"Maybe Mr. Frond is waiting in the closet to see if we will behave," someone said. That sentence completely froze me in my tracks. I was not getting up anymore. We waited for another 15 minutes. Finally, someone snapped, and it was none other than Byron Franks.

"There is NO-oo teacher coming! We are sitting here, being perfect, for NOTHING!"

Everyone stared at Byron.

"But what if he is listening to us?" Pleaded Phoebe.

"How would he? He is absent!"

We all stared blankly at him, silently begging for him to sit back down.

"He IS NOT HERE, what don't you get?"

He stormed to the front of the room, and sat on the teacher's desk. We all stared at him in pure terror.

"Still not enough?" He put his feet on the desk. We were frozen, all of us had heard since we first started school that Mr. Frond was the scariest teacher ever, and Byron of all kids, was denying it?

"Oh come on! You know what, I'll prove it. I'll open your stupid cabinet!" He walked to the large metal cabinet and pulled on the lever. The door opened to reveal an old man, with a long white beard and black-rimmed glasses.

"Oh thank you for letting me out, I got stuck in the cabinet before class. Heh."

Everyone in class's mouth gaped open, but none larger than Byron's. We knew it plausible that he may be listening to us, but to *actually* have been in the closet?

He walked to the center of the room. As soon as he turned towards us, Byron made a mad dash towards his desk.

"Hello class, I am your Latin teacher, Mr. Frond."

* * *

Mr. Frond was everyone's favorite teacher. He has been pranking 6th graders like us for 4 decades. Every Latin student was to keep his joke a secret, and as more time passed, the funnier it got.

" I got the idea from a student I had 43 years ago." He explained. "She told the grade below her I was horrible because I had given her a B instead of an A on some test. Her name was Lauren Wallace. You may have heard of her." Mrs. Wallace was the superintendent of The Coventry Garden School.

He was a mentor for all of us. Surprisingly, he especially liked me. Right before Winter break we had an assignment to make a poster about an animal in latin. He had a book that, I might add he had written, where it had information about almost every animal in Latin, and English translation right underneath. He even allowed us to just copy it onto a poster. I did the Wolf, and I never expected I would learn so much from this project as I did. I wouldn't say much of this is super useful, but I can tell you a lot about the Wolf in Latin. He told me it was one of the best posters he had ever had for this project, which he had been doing for 40 years. He called me Ludus from then on. (Ludus is wolf in Latin) I had him through 8th grade, but since he was getting old, he had not taught 9th through 11th in a few years.

We have a different Latin teacher this year, Ms. Cooper, and Mr. Frond has tried to make the impression on even her that the rumors are true. On the last day of 8th grade he told us, "Tell Ms. Cooper I am as mean as the rumors say. I'll tell her the truth when I retire." I still visit Mr. Frond almost every day. He helps me out a lot. He knows everything about me. Everything except the fact that I am cursed and my father *is* the devil.

* * *

It is nearly Thanksgiving break, and I am discussing with Coley our math test results. He got an A. I got a C.

"How come you always get good grades when you don't even try and when I study for 5 hours a day I do terribly? I am going to be kicked out of special math soon," I asked.

"No, you won'," he said.

"Yes, I will and you know it," I replied.

"You're just being hard on yourself," Coley said.

The door to the study hall suddenly swings open and I see a disheveled girl standing there. Our study hall teacher walks up to her. They talk for a little, and she goes and sits down 5 feet away from me.

"Who's that?" I ask Coley.

It takes him a minute to recognize her. "Oh, I think that's Elizabeth. I haven't seen her all year."

The lunch bell rings nearly immediately after.

"Yeah"

CHAPTER 4

I take a deep breath to steady my nerves, my whole body aching with a mixture of fear and nervous excitement. She is sitting alone on the slide contemplating her notebook. Nobody is taking a second glance at her or bothering to talk to her. I am going to change this today. At least I hope I will. I had thought it would be easy to quickly walk up to strike up a conversation but it had become much different the second I had decided to actually go and talk to her. I stood there for a good five minutes as still as if there was a wasp right by me waiting to sting me.

I finally decided that I could not do it. I turned back towards the cafeteria ready to eat all the ice cream that I could so I could soak in my misery. On my way to the cafeteria, I accidentally bumped into Darcy. He glared at me and shoved me out of the way, stomping his way over towards Elizabeth. Now the only good thing about this dreary school was that recess and lunch were a good two hours. I made my way to the cafeteria to see Coley sitting excitedly at the same table we had just ate lunch while waiting to hear how my incredible chat with Elizabeth went. I walked right by him, however, giving him as much of a gaze as I would give a plate full of salad. I continued walking straight to the lunch line getting as much ice cream as would fit in my pudgy stomach.

I went back to Coley, still not speaking, eating my ice cream in depressed silence. I ate my ice cream so fast it felt as if I had inhaled it rather than swallowed it. I then went back out to the playground to see Elizabeth still sitting on the slide, nonchalantly swiping the pages of her notebook, as Darcy walked away in an angry huff.

All of a sudden however she got up and rushed from the playground. I followed her of course, her emotions were hard to make out, but I could feel them and they were very strong. She was walking towards the fence, which was confusing, but then she veered off to the left taking a more unexpected route towards the bushes right on the perimeter of the school. I continued to follow her and then saw her climb into the bush, her face gripped, fighting through the pain of all the little thorns pricking her sides. The bushes seemingly swallowed her as she disappeared into the depths beyond. I began running knowing that if I wanted to find out what she was doing I was going to have to hurry.

I reached the bush and stopped for a moment. I searched for a moment and then quickly found the small opening in which Elizabeth had gone through. I forced myself through the opening, in doing so feeling like an overweight monkey, and then suddenly, as I pushed myself one last time finally to the end of the hole, I began falling. I fell for just a few seconds, but it still felt like an eternity. My body was in such a state of shock that when I tried to let out a scream just a rather feeble burp came out. This may however have been a good thing because the less conspicuous I was the better. Suddenly the falling stopped.

It was rather unsettling when I hit the ground, not only because I had no idea what I would land on, which appeared to be a soft, somehow liquid-solid that made me want to barf, but that would not be a good look. I got up, still very shaken, and then suddenly I realized that my eyes were still closed. I must have closed them as I was falling and now I opened them ready to see what habitat I had so very graciously intruded on. As I opened my eyes it was as if the sun had suddenly been brought down from space and put in the room. My eyes burned for a moment but as they adjusted to the light I began to have a general relaxation of my surroundings. What I saw at first was shining silver walls and a map stuck in the back corner by a desk and then directly across from that was a cot. It looked as if it were made of stone. I decided to then see if the cot really was made of stone. I worked my way over despite the searing of my eyes, I felt the bed with my hand and though it wasn't made of stone it certainly wasn't a mattress.

Suddenly there was a shocked gasp from behind and a horrified voice shouting

"How did you get in here?" she shouted.

I looked back to find Elizabeth angry and confused. She was shouting at me. I stammered for a moment, nearly lost my footing, regained my balance by grabbing the cot behind me and in doing so lost my balance again. I fell on the cot and everything went black.

I woke up sweating. I was very confused as to where I was and why there were no pumpkins trying to attack me with sporks. So I shouted:

"Come out and fight!! Your sporks do not scare me!"

Suddenly Elizabeth came into view looking even more confused than I was and I realized I had been dreaming. I was so embarrassed I could have let the rocky cot I laid upon cave in on me, never to be seen again. Elizabeth seemed to assume that I had been dreaming as she came beside the cot with an ice pack and placed it on my head.

"So, what are you doing here?" She asked again.

"Um, well I followed you," I responded nervously.

"Really?" She said looking surprised.

"Yeah, I saw you sitting alone on the slide so I thought I might try and talk to you and then you started walking off towards the bushes and well, it's not like I won't follow someone who shimmies through a hole in a tiny patch of bushes," I admitted.

She laughed and then asked, "Your name is Preston right?"

"Yes," I responded.

"Well, nice to meet you Preston, my name is Elizabeth."

* * *

"So, why do you live down here?" I asked.

Elizabeth looked at me suddenly with a puzzled look and I could see the struggle and the contradiction behind whatever she was thinking.

"You know when I was younger, I knew someone named Preston," she said.

"Really? I knew someone named Elizabeth when I was younger as well," I said.

"Interesting," she said with a skeptical look on her face.

I could see her make a decision in her eyes and then she started to speak.

"Something terrible happened to that boy I knew. Something terrible indeed. I am not sure if you believe in devils, but I used to work with one. Not only did I work with one, but I also helped one. During that period of time when I worked with The Devil, he cursed that boy named Preston. He cursed him in an awful way indeed," she explained

My mouth went dry and my mouth dropped below my knees.

CHAPTER 5

Preston hesitated for a fraction of a second, before he said, uncertainly:

"Yes."

It was worth a shot. She placed her hand on the cold stone wall and felt its porous surface beneath her skin.

"Put your hand on the wall. Next to mine," she instructed.

Looking vaguely confused, Preston obeyed.

The stone grew warm.

From deep within came a faint pulse, like a heartbeat.

With a grinding, crushing sound of rock against rock, the wall rearranged itself to form the entrance to a tunnel, large enough for the two of them.

"Follow me."

The boy did so, appearing almost comically shocked.

As soon as they had crossed over the threshold, the wall reformed behind them, as though the gaping mouth had never been there at all, throwing them into inky darkness. For a moment, Preston fumbled for a light switch, and his hand slipped into Elizabeth's cool, firm grip.

"This way."

Her booted footfalls clicked off the stone as she led him deeper and deeper into the depths of the cavern. They walked in silence along the path, gradually sloping downwards, for what could have been an eternity or a matter of minutes.

As his other hand brushed against the wall, Preston felt it move.

A wave of terror washed over him, and he had the sudden, intense urge to flee, to escape whatever great beast had just swallowed him whole. A drop of something wet and acidic landed with a *plunk* on his head.

"W - Where are we?"

"You'll see."

A small, colorless, warmthless flame flickered into being in the palm of Elizabeth's hand. She blew gently on it, and it shot forward.

One by one, the rows of wooden torches along the wall, set in sconces of dark metal, ignited, crackling with a pale viridian light.

They were in a narrow passage, with smooth, damp walls hewn of black stone. The shadows cast across the floor loomed, malevolent and alien, a mockery of humanoid form. In his peripheral vision, Preston was sure he saw them move independent of any action on his part, writhing and coiling, fingers elongated into tendrils of darkness, mouths becoming leering, sharp-toothed grimaces.

Quickly releasing Preston's hand, Elizabeth turned to face him.

"So, how *did* you find your way to my humble abode?"

"As I mentioned, I may or may not have been following you."

She smiled. "How charming. And what is so fascinating about me that you follow my every move?"

"More than you know," he said, gravely.

"Please enlighten me."

"I have been watching you for a while, Elizabeth Grey. When I arrived here a year ago and saw you, I couldn't shake the feeling that we had met before. There was something familiar about you, I guess, that made you so intriguing. You're so... look, I, well..."

As they came around a corner, the faint sound of voices reached Preston's ears, coming from farther along the snaking corridor. Letting his previous sentence trail off into nothingness, he said, again:

"Elizabeth? Where are you taking me?"

"To see my family. Almost there now."

Preston stared at her, confused. What family could she possibly have down there, deep in the bowels of the earth?

As the space around them gradually opened up into a small stone room, the final torches lit of their own accord, illuminating what lay at the far end.

The door was a monstrosity of creation, a twisted, gnarled behemoth of iron and strange black stone. It had no handle and was decorated with a scene out of a nightmare.

Countless women and children lay in varying states of prostration at the foot of a great cube, inlaid with precious gems, their faces smooth, featureless. Perched like some loathsome bird on top of the cube was one of the strangest creatures Preston had ever seen. Though most of the figure was shrouded in the sagging folds of a voluminous yellow-painted cloak, what was visible was all the more terrifying. Long thin limbs, batlike in their fragility, extended from the cloak's depths, innumerable and grasping.

Through a slit in the center of the cloak, a golden rib cage, bare and sharpened, gaped. Suckered tendrils, scaled like the tails of snakes, coiled around its sides, some lifting these women into the air, towards the thing's head, wrinkled, regal, and only vaguely human, surmounted by a crown of magnificent gilded antlers. Hair cascaded down its shoulders like oily gray streams. Loose skin hung and sagged in odd places, like a poorly fitting rubber mask. Row after row of needle-like teeth jutted from a yawning, frog-like mouth, a four-foot tongue lolling out of one edge. Set into the sides of this face, which protruded from the rest of the carving as though breaching the waters separating it from reality, were two pale blue stones, like chips of ice. They seemed to be staring at Preston, reaching slick, oily tentacles beneath his skin and into his mind.

Come - closer - closer - hungry, so hungry - **starving** ***so long - cold - need - FEEEED ME.***

Preston stared at it, and slowly extended his hand, face slack, eyes glassy and staring, mouth open in reverence.

"Preston?"

His small, pale hand reached the creature's razor-toothed mouth and entered it, disappearing entirely from view.

As the teeth broke his skin, he awoke from his trance with a cry, and his blood ran down in rivulets, through a series of cataracts and indentations, finally collecting in a small sacrificial bowl at the base, outstretched in the arms of one of the stone women.

Like a cold glass filled suddenly with scalding liquid, the bowl cracked in two, raining crimson droplets across the floor, spreading through the gaps between tiles, a sanguine labyrinth beneath their feet. The cold eyes of the statue settled on Preston's heart.

Welcome home, boy.

Clutching his ears as though to block out some painful sound inaudible to Elizabeth beside him, Preston fell to his knees, cradling his injured hand.

When he opened his eyes again, he realized with a start that he had been screaming, and saw Elizabeth staring at him, wide-eyed. How long had he been that way? Seconds? Minutes? Hours upon hours?

"What is this - what is this place? Where have you taken me?" he demanded shakily, standing unsteadily, voice quavering.

"This, Preston, is my home, where I have lived since I was three."

"Why did you take me here? What- lives-"

He looked terrified, lips thin, eyes bulging from their sockets, feral like a cornered rabbit. His hand, from which a steady stream of blood was flowing, looked as though he had used it to break through a glass window.

And he was gone, bolting, sprinting down the tunnel, droplets of blood flying from his pumping arm.

"Preston!" She called after him, without much hope. His footfalls began to recede.

Sighing, Elizabeth sat down on a large rock next to the statue to think.

She had seen Preston around Coventry, though their classes were entirely separate. He was a shy, quiet child, with few to confide in, which whom she sympathized with. Who could he tell?

There was that other boy, but Preston would not tell him anything. Yes, he would never tell, and if he did, it would be her word against his. If it came to it, no one would notice if he was gone for a few days, which would be quite adequate. She doubted even his parents paid much heed to him, a pale wisp of a boy with a mop of mousy brown hair, provided he *had* parents. He often gave off the appearance of having slept in the woods bordering the school, and she sometimes caught glimpses of a stray leaf or dirt stuck to him.

Elizabeth scowled. Why must her first thought always be of murder? The boy knew nothing. All that he had seen could be explained away, rendered trivial. She had nothing to worry about.

The statue grinned at her obscenely from its perch, a challenge.

"Oh, leave me alone."

She stood up, wiping the ancient dust off of her jeans, and put her hand on the massive door.

Soundlessly, it swung open on its titanic hinges, the white light oozing through the widening crack squirming like a grumble of swollen maggots bursting from beneath the thin skin of a vegetable left to fester in the beating sun.

Elizabeth Gray had a job to do. But first, there was someone she needed to see, an old friend who waited on the other side.

She stepped into the light and was gone.

CHAPTER 6

I methodically work my way back down the tunnel darkness paving my path back to Elizabeth's... home or lair. I am not sure what it is but I keep going towards it knowing that I can find my way out somehow, if I can find that room. I flinch again for what seems to be the 40th time in the past minute as somehow despite it having been so quiet down here earlier it seems as if the underworld had awoken and I was intruding on these unknown beings' waking hours. I begin to run. I have a disturbing feeling that the longer I stay here, the more danger I am in.

My footsteps echo against the walls as I get closer to Elizabeth's room, the steel walls sensing my approach. I reach the opening to her room and hesitate for a moment. I wonder if I have made a mistake running away from this meeting that Elizabeth wanted me to join but I know I have made the right choice. I keep moving, slowing my pace to a more lingering movement, careful with each step attempting to make as little noise as possible and to sense any impending danger. I look around the room for a moment. The lights are still on and nothing seems to have changed since Elizabeth and I have last been here, but it certainly feels empty. I grasp in my mind for a moment a recollection of some connection between me and Elizabeth or maybe me and this meeting but it's gone in a second lost in a wisp of silence, eaten by the underworld.

I shake my head aggravated with myself that I would let such precious time to escape, slip out of my fingertips. I immediately move towards the vicinity of where I had entered the room when I had first crawled through these bushes. I can see the mud and dirt that I had fallen into when I landed but there is no way I could possibly get back to land this way as well. I pout for a moment wanting to believe that I could be possibly trapped in this solitary confinement with Elizabeth forever but I know better. If Elizabeth lives down here or has been down here enough to create a living space then she has to have a way of bringing herself back to mere humanity.

I look for a lever or a big red button perhaps with a sign screaming "Push me to go back to the real world!" But I have no such luck. I check all around Elizabeth's room checking everywhere there could be a glimpse of jumping up to earth but still no luck. I push against cracks in walls and small crevices maybe leading to an opening but no secret door eradicates itself from the wall. I go back to the muddy pit that I fell into what seems like days ago and walk inside. I move around the walls which look as if they were carved out creating the perfect space for a portal to the underground and then I walk to the middle of the mud and sit down as angry as a four year old who didn't get his Oreos. The second I sit down, the floor begins to push me upwards. As I lurch upwards I look around at the walls spinning with giant fans pushing the now floating circle of dirt and mud with ease. I laugh hysterically. The perfect storybook ending to my expedition to the underworld.

I push myself through the bushes going out back to the playground this time. Cold dark air fills my lungs and body. It's as if the air is telling me something awful has happened. I grit my teeth and walk towards the main doors hoping the day isn't over yet because I need to find Coley. The doors are locked like I expected. They're always locked during the school day; the only way they open is from the inside or the teachers can open the doors from the outside with their teacher I.Ds. It must be my lucky day as when I look through the windows the halls are overflowing with students, it must be passing time. I pound on the glass knowing at least one kind soul will open the doors and let me inside and someone does almost immediately. I can see the sullen look on the boy's face even as he comes to open the door for me. I don't recognize the boy but I do wonder why he could be so sullen.

I walk into the building, warmth finding a way back to me and I look at a clock on the wall. It's 2:15, 7th period, the last period of the day. My timing could not be any better. I have period 7 math with Coley. I navigate the halls as if I have photocopied a map of the school into my brain, focused intently on making it to math. I walk into the classroom triumphantly feeling as if I have won an Olympic gold medal until Coley is all of a sudden in my face whispering at me. "Where have you been??" he yells softly "I have been scared for your life especially since what happened to John." "What happened to John?" I whisper back. He motions his head toward the door and I understand what he means. It's still passing time and at this point, I don't even care if I am marked missing for another class.

We march out of the door in unison. We both know where to go. The faculty cafeteria is closed to all teachers and students during 7th period for cleaning but we know the janitors never bother to clean it so it's always free. We check to make sure nobody is watching us as we enter the faculty cafeteria though just as a cautionary, we both know no one is going to see us. We enter and walk towards the munchkin box on the table and each takes a jelly filled before either of us talk. He starts talking first.

"Listen, I don't know how you haven't heard this yet or where you have been since recess but," I cut him off.

"Listen, I am sure that whatever happened to John is terrible and whatever but I need to tell you something, like right now."

He looks at me suspiciously and gives an unexpected remark saying, "Well, you will find out about John soon enough.

There is going to be an assembly on it this period." "Well, then I'll find out then but let me tell you where I went during recess before it's too late. I have a bad feeling that whatever happened down there was dangerous."

I begin to recount my very non-stalkerish following of Elizabeth down into the underworld and how I pushed myself through a hole the size of Coley's head just to fall 20 feet into a bunch of mud and dirt. I began to explain to him the emptiness and solitude of this room that I had fallen into but it was nearly impossible to put into words. I lighten my voice as I get to the part where I feel rendering myself unconscious, rather embarrassed when all of a sudden an alarm sounds. Coley seems unfazed by the alarm, as if he was expecting it whereas I nearly fall out of my seat. Coley gets up looking at me expectantly saying "Ready?" Only then do I realize that the assembly bell is what's ringing.

"No, we can't go, I am just getting to the important stuff, Coley." He looks at me with a pained expression on his face

"We have to go Preston, you'll see why as soon as we're there."

We sprint down the hall towards the auditorium not wanting to be late, already at a disadvantage due to the teachers' cafeteria being much further away than all classrooms. We catch up to a class lagging behind the others and snake onto the end of the line hoping to draw as little attention as possible. The teacher is taking roll call as they walk which gives us an explanation as to why this class is so much further behind all others but aggravates us nonetheless.

We enter the auditorium and head towards the middle seating area and take two seats neither directly next to another person. I look up towards the sunshine lit stage to see a screen with John's face covering it. I push back the urge to again ask Coley what in the world is going on as I know he will just respond by saying that everything will be explained in the assembly. In an instant, Mr. Frond is on stage and I almost burst out laughing as he puts on his show of being the worst, strictest teacher in the world while he introduces the headmaster Dr. Chalice.

Dr. Chalice comes onstage walking as straight as she can for being in heels and she doesn't do too badly. She finds the microphone and pulls it from its stand. "Students, I am sure almost every single one of you has already heard this news but, to those of you who do not know already, a great tragedy has occurred today. Not just in our school, but also our community. This morning at 8:53 A.M on March 13th John Derusa's mother dialed 101 after having gone into her son's room to wake him up for the school day and finding blood dripping from the sheets of his bed and a knife in his stomach." Cries ring out bouncing from wall to wall in the auditorium, awakening the demons inside them.

Dr. Chalice quiets the crowd with a soft hush into the microphone. "Before the police arrived however, Mrs. Rerusa discovered that there was also a suicide note found on John's left arm which as John's mother was crying hysterically, was not written in John's handwriting. When the police arrived and brought John to the hospital he was named dead within two minutes of inspection." I take a sharp intake cutting off Dr. Chalice and her robotic, cold explanation of John's gruesome death.

Everyone has always known that Dr. Chalice had seemed to have no emotions but this seemed to take it to the next level. Her ability to robotically explain the details of a 13 year olds gruesome suicide is horrifying. "This suicide note glued to John's arm with blood seemed to be a clear explanation of John's death but police decided to investigate further in an attempt to either confirm the suicide or call foul play. The police found multiple pieces of evidence that there was another person in John's room with him the night of his apparent suicide such as two pairs of footsteps traveling from John's door to his bed stopping at his bed moving around a bit and then making their way back out of John's room. There was also a bit of leather found on the floor near some of these footsteps. It was confirmed by John's mother that not a single piece of leather can be found in the Derusa household. Using this evidence and other smaller clues not worthy of my explanation, the police have decided to launch a full-scale investigation into the death of John Derusa and not a single student shall leave the grounds of this school unless they wish to be taken into custody by the police."

CHAPTER 7

I rose from my seat with shivers going down my spine. I could feel the hairs and goosebumps rising on my arms and at the back of the neck. What vile person would ever dare kill someone? Or well, make him want to kill himself. I never really knew John, but Elizabeth did. I remember seeing them laugh while walking to class together. I can't really picture him committing suicide. He seemed like a happy guy. Good grades, lots of friends, not so many enemies or at least as many as I originally thought. I guess him doing this really showed how much of a mask our faces can be. And Elizabeth, well, she's probably devastated. Speaking of her, where is she? I didn't see her walking inside of the auditorium, then again it was probably her who left with a cry once his fate was revealed. Gosh, I'm being told of the death of a student and I can seem to think about Elizabeth!

Staying beside Coley as I walked out of the big room of students, we went straight past the stone hallways and outside since we were relieved of classes for the rest of the day. A couple of other kids seemed to think the same way since we passed them, but others (mostly friends of John, may he rest in peace) went to their dorms. Probably bawling their eyes out and using every single tissue in the building.

Coley and I walked past tall pine trees and sat down on a bench. The silence that filled the conversation broke after a couple minutes.

"Do you really think he committed suicide?" Coley asked me.

"I don't know Coley anymore. He was a pretty popular guy. Of course, popularity can give you a bunch of jealous kids that dedicate their lives to making yours terrible. But I only thought that was in movies, I never expected it to make him feel that bad. So bad that it made him end his life," I replied looking at nothing in particular.

"So you're saying that suicide was their cover-up?"

"Yes, no. I mean, if it was a suicide, then it was a very tragic loss for the school spirit. But if it was, I don't know, murder, then he must have done something terrible. Something that would have ended with him in a bad situation." I spoke with a clear voice. "You?" I looked at him. He was shaking in his seat.

"Whatever happened, it ended with the death of a student, a kid. It sucks." He said honestly. I turned my attention back to the green sight in front of me. "But I'm going to go back to our dorm, you coming?" he asked me. I squinted my eyes to a tree, there was a girl behind it, peeking over at me. Elizabeth.

"You go ahead. I need a long breath of air, but I'll catch up." I ushered him. He just nodded his head and left as I got up and walked over to Elizabeth. She saw me coming over to her and hid behind the tree. I leaned my back and headed to the opposite side of the tree. I could hear her breath get tangled and her loud heart beating quickly.

"You know, if you wanted to talk to me you could have just walked over to me," I told her.

"You were with Coley," she replied quietly.

"But I'm free now, care to take a walk?"

"Sure," she replied. I put my arm out and she wrapped hers around it. "I know a nice path in the forest. I promise it's not a dark and scary maze."

"I'm sorry about that. I didn't mean to leave you alone there. It just seemed, this sounds so weird, but familiar in a way. And that's what scared me. Not you, not ever. Nothing you do will ever scare me." I assured her. She just scrunched her nose and mumbled something under her breath. "What?" I asked.

"I said that you never being scared of things I do is debatable. I've done some scary stuff," I laughed.

"Like what? Tell me." She stopped abruptly and looked me in the eyes, deciding if she could trust me as I trusted her.

"Well, when I was five I ate a worm," I grinned.

"We all did that Liz"

"Well I also climbed to the top of a tree, I was practicing a, umm...hobby. And something came crashing into me. I fell down onto my back. I was unconscious for a whole week. I was seven." She told me. I gaped.

"Wow, that must have been terrifying."

" It was." I could tell that a story of mine was needed.

"This isn't so scary as much as disturbing, but when I was little I once drank a whole bottle of red paint. When my mom found me she thought I was bleeding. She went crazy." I sighed at the memory of my mother. It had been so long.

" What was your mom like?" Elizabeth asked me. I made a small smile.

"I haven't seen her in a long time. But she had dark brown eyes and hair like mine, only much longer. She acted happily, always wore a smile. But I could tell it in her eyes, she was sad. I don't know why I never had the courage to ask. But every once and a while, they weren't sad. They were genuinely happy. Those days were the best. We would go get ice cream and spend the day at the beach. Depending on the weather that day. If not we would do other stuff. Rock climbing, going to see movies. You get the point." She nodded her head.

"Do you still talk?" I thought about the new question she asked.

" No. I- she's not dead, as far as I know, but we haven't spoken in a couple of years. Big fight right before I left for school. And I really don't know what she's doing now."

"I know what it's like losing someone close. Whether it's to the inevitable end of their time, or to a fight like you and your mom."

"My condolences on John by the way," I said. "you guys were pretty close if I'm right."

"Ya, we were." She sniffled and wiped her nose on the bottom of her uniform shirt. "He was a good friend. Always there if you needed him, always willing to give you his things. Gosh, I miss him." She sat down on a moss-covered stump. I sat down on the log beside her. Hesitantly, I wrapped my arms around her. She flinched as I did so, but after a second she returned the hug. I pulled her tighter, showing her that I was there for her.

"Thank you, Preston."

"I know I can't replace John, but I'm here. I trust you, I'm going to be here even if everyone else is against you."

"Once again, debatable," she says.

"Why do you say that?" I ask her.

"I've done unforgivable things. Stuff that haunts me sometimes." I sat straighter.

"Elizabeth, whatever you do, you can tell me, I can't judge you."

"Opinions change," she said loudly as she stood up. "I'm not the perfect schoolgirl, the girl who always gets good grades. She's a FAKE. You need to understand that not everything is as it seems." She yelled at me. I've never seen her like this.

"No Elizabeth, I know you, I've watched you for years. I've paid so much attention to you that I know you better than I even know myself," I argued back.

"Well, you're wrong." Her voice was very loud. I wouldn't be surprised if people back at the school heard her.

"Tell me how I'm wrong. Please, enlighten me!" I spoke sarcastically. "What is so bad that Elizabeth Gray, the girl who owns my heart, thinks she is so terrible, so cruel, so evil," I spoke so loud, my throat hurt. But it didn't seem as if Elizabeth's was the same.

"Because I did it." She screamed. Her shiny hair was now knotted, messy because of all the pulling she did on it.

"Did what?" I asked her quietly now. "Elizabeth what did you do?" I grabbed her by the shoulders. "Please tell me," I whispered. She turned her head to the side, looking away from me. Her previously teary eyes were now red-stained. The features on her face made it so that you knew she was angry.

"I killed him" Her voice was as clear as day. As unfazed as an arrow in the wind. I gasped and let go of her shoulders. I took a couple of steps back.

"Killed who?" She tilted her head towards me.

"I think you know," she said to me. And she was right. I did know who.

"John. You killed John. It wasn't suicide. You just made it look like it." She broke out into a sickly sweet smile.

"Yes, I did. Now tell me, Preston, are you still not scared of me? Do you still trust me after hearing my truth? Do you still want me to own your heart? Are you scared that I'll do it again, or are you positive you can trust me not to?"

She took a step towards me and I fell back. I quickly got up and ran back to the school, leaving Elizabeth to watch me go. At this moment it was branded in gold in my mind.

Elizabeth Grey, my love, was the murderer of John DeRusa.

CHAPTER 8

Running back to my dorm room, my heart was beating so fast it was humming, I couldn't calm down. I was having trouble breathing. I changed my pace to a run, knowing that if someone found me in this state there would be no end to my questioning. I ran up the dorm stairs, into Coley and my room; room 1478-B.

"Preston! Oh my gosh, where were you?!" Coley was sitting in his bed, his face painted with loads of worry. He sprang up from the bed and scrambled over to me making sure I was alright.

"Coley, I-I'm fine, Ok? I'm g-good," I said, looking at Coley with the most 'I'm Ok' look I could give, but my answer obviously didn't satisfy him.

"PRESTON! You're stuttering! Get into your clothes and I'll make some tea. Ok?" Coley led me to my bed, and set me under the covers. As he was making the tea, all I could think about was my 'meeting' with Elizabeth. She killed someone. The beautiful angel that I had once known, --or thought I'd known--was all wrong.

"She murdered somebody, she took a knife and was all like; BAM! Into the gut, blood, blood, blood, and then BOOM! They're dead. Oh god. How could someone do that?" I thought. My face was creased with lines of worry and confusement.

"Woah there, Soldier! It looks like you've got so much on your mind your head is bulging!" I looked up to see Coley smiling down at me. He had the tea in his hand, and had sugar cookies in the other.

"Thanks, Coley. Yeah, my meeting with Elizabeth was a bit nerve racking," I said not wanting to bring up the conversation again.

"Well Preston, all times are scary now I suppose. But I thought you liked Elizabeth. Remember when you used to ramble about her 'blood red lips', and how 'devilishly beautiful" she was?" Coley asked, acting like Elizabeth at each time he described her.

"Blood red lips. She's done this before," I said, then realizing I said it out loud.

"By gosh, what has she done more than once? Come on Pres, you ain't going to leave your old pal, Coley in the dirt right? You're gonna tell him what's goin' on right? ...Preston?"

He was on the brink of tears, and then I could see. Coley was scared, scared of getting murdered, but mostly scared that I would get hurt. If I didn't tell him, he would never know how to protect me. But I couldn't tell him. I don't know what consequences it would bring, and I didn't want to know. I promised myself I was doing this for HIM.

"Just... I can't Coley, I wish I could but I can't. I'm going to bed," I said. Coley looked saddened, and betrayed, but I knew that I couldn't tell him. Besides, I was so tired, I needed to sleep...

"Preston... Preston! Hurry you, imbecile, I don't have much time here." Someone was talking to me. I jerked awake, or what I thought was awake to see fire in the form of a human standing over me. He pressed his hand over my head, and I was transported.

Surrounding me was fire, lava, and black figures flying ahead. Ahead of me was a throne, and sitting on it was the most mischievous looking person I had ever met.

"Welcome to my humble home; Hell. Close your mouth Preston. You will wake up soon, and so I don't have much time."

'I'm asleep?" I was confused. I thought I had died, and I ended up in Hell.

"Do try and keep up... You see Preston our little problem here is that you almost spilled Elizabeth's confession to Coley, your mortal friend correct? So, if you want to keep your little friend alive, I recommend you keep the murder a secret."

"How do you know about that!?" I asked. All of this was so confusing.

"Simple Preston, simple. One, I am the God of Fire and Death, so naturally, I know. Second of all, Elizabeth, well... She has very special privileges."

"What is that supposed to mean?" I asked. Killing someone was not a special privilege. This guy made absolutely no sense.

"Ignorant boy, you have wasted all my time with you dumb questions. My proclamation is simple boy! If you want to keep Coley, SHUT YOUR DAMN MOUTH!"

It was dark, and I was sweaty. Everything was swirling around my head, and I couldn't keep myself controlled. Everything was blurry, my life, my mind, everything I owned that made me, me.

"*Coley...,*" I thought I had to make sure he was alright. When I looked at Coley's bed, I could have sworn he wasn't there, but somehow he came back. But it was just my eyes deceiving me.

And what that fiery man had said, I swore, on my own life that I would never tell a soul.

CHAPTER 9

"The story of that poor village is horrible....because it is true!"

As much as I love Mr. Frond, he just over exaggerates what he teaches too much. And yes, I know it is out of enthusiasm for Latin history or whatnot, but it gets on your nerves when you're not in the mood for it. And I was not in the mood for it.

He was talking about an old village that could have been the capital instead of Rome, but had an infestation problem with rats, and it wound up abandoned, because most of the inhabitants died of disease, and a bunch of other unimportant details that I don't know how the world even knows about. But point blank, I was in a bad mood and his lecture was pissing me off.

The entire day I had been dozing off into the deep depths of my mind, trying to stay away from *other* thoughts, and frankly, it was not helping me at all. For all I could conclude, it was probably hurting my goal more than helping.

"Ok class, you can go a few minutes early," he said after seeing most of the class was disengaged. I began to walk off, until he motioned me back to him.

"Just a second Preston, but could you come here?" I trudged on over to him, wishing he could have chosen a better day to summon me to his desk.

"Dr. Chalice would like to speak with you Preston. She told me to send you, so please head up to her office now."

"Why specifically?"

"Go Preston," he said. Something was up. But I went anyway.

The administrators building had a circular entrance with fancy paintings on the wall. There were doors everywhere, but only one desk. The desk was in the corner of the room with one of the administrators sitting in it.

"Are you Preston?" the administrator asked rudely. I nodded. "Go into Dr. Chalices office now."

I walked towards the door with Dr. Chalice's name on it. The closer I got, the more nervous I became. I had never been in Dr. Chalice's office before. Dr. Chalice was a cold and emotionless person. She was good at her job, but not someone you want to be on your bad side. I wasn't even sure why I was on her bad side.

I knocked before entering, and slowly opened the door. Inside sat Dr. Chalice, her gaze penetrating through my skin.

"Hello Preston," she emitted no emotion with those words.

"Good afternoon Dr. Chalice," I said nervously. I was now trembling, and I didn't know why.

"Preston. Let me put it plain and simple. Do you know *anything* about the murder of John DeRusa?" She stared at me with her blank expression.

Quick, what do I say? "Outside of your knowledge?" I ask, immediately angry at myself for such a foolish response.

"Yes, outside of my knowledge. Don't play dumb," she said, irritated.

I hesitate for a moment, and then state, "I have heard a rumor that it was a hired murder, but I don't know much past what the police has said."

"Oh is that so Preston? And *who* exactly did you hear this rumor from? I do know you lack many friends," she grinned menacingly.

Rats. "I heard it from Coley, who is my friend. He said he heard it during...art class, yeah art class. He heard some kids gossiping about it" I said. I didn't *want* to throw Coley under the bus with me, but I was kind of in a hole right here.

"I see," she thought for a moment, swiveling in her fancy roller chair. "Let me tell you a story, Preston. A story from just 20 years ago. In this. very. spot."

"Please do."

Now, I thought I was getting on her nerves, but she brushed it off like a piece of sand.

"Before this was my office, this spot was a little pond. There were some small trees, flowers on the grass, and a couple of benches; it really was a lovely spot. 22 years ago, a boy named Arthur Canden came to Coventry Garden, and from day one, he sat by the pond every day. He was new to the school as a 9th grader. But he didn't just blend in with the crowd. He was all bones, quite wacky looking I must admit. The entire school seemed to bully him, they bullied him every day. My fellow teachers and I could do nothing to stop it, for it was so widespread. My office at the time was down a few hundred yards east, and it had a lovely view of the pond. And every morning, at around 6, when I would get to work, I would see Arthur Canden sitting on the bench and looking at the fish. Every day. He could just brush all of that bullying off like it was nothing."

She stopped for a moment, fully immersed in her story.

"No one ever came into the pond anymore. It was just Arthur and the fish. But then, one day in late November, someone else came into the pond. It was a girl I had seen once before, but the one time I had seen her was with the group of kids who bullied Arthur. I expected her to bully him, and the rest of her friends to show up right behind her. But instead, she apologized. She apologized for all of her friends that were part of the group that was the rudest towards him. Sure, I couldn't actually hear what she had said, but she had definitely apologized. From then on, I would see them both sitting at that pond. Almost every day she would be there with him. They became best friends. I never saw her with the bullies anymore. She became an outcast as well. For 3 months, through the cold I would see them at that pond in the morning."

She looked over at me for the first time since she started the story.

"You probably think I'm a stalker. And I guess with him, I was. I never talked to Arthur once, but I knew almost everything about him just from seeing him at that pond. And, from my duties as headmaster, of course." She paused for a few seconds. "You want to know something funny? I didn't know who the girl actually was. And sure, I had access to everything about anyone in the school, and if I had wanted to I could see who she was in a heartbeat. But I just didn't."

"But one Monday in late February, February 24th to be exact, I showed up at my office, and Arthur wasn't there. The next day neither of them showed up again, and I got worried. I checked on the attendance records, and Arthur had missed all of his classes those past two days. He was missing! The police came, and they found him. But they found him dead. Dead at the bottom of the pond."

She stopped, a tear in her eye.

"Everyone thought at first that it was a murder commited by one of the bullies. The largest suspect was a boy named Harrison Halton. The cops sat with him for hours, but he wouldn't confess. He insisted he did not do it. They were about to send him to the slam house when, found in the mail, was a note sent by Arthur, and it was addressed to someone named Josephine Drew."

She stopped again, consoling herself. This story is getting really awkward, I have got to admit. It feels like Dr. Chalice is just telling the story to herself, and I'm just a bystander.

"That was the girl who was his only friend. The case was closed, and everything was supposed to go back to normal. But I didn't buy it. If I had learned anything from seeing him at that pond everyday, it was he cared about life, no matter how bad. So I went into detective mode. I looked through all of the files on who bullied him, attendance records, and his personal information. But then, I looked at the surveillance video. Sure, the cops looked through Sundays, and Monday's video, but I wasn't sure if they had looked through Friday's or Saturday's.

"The first night I dedicated myself to video scanning, it went by without anything. But, the next morning, I picked up right where I had left off. Just five minutes of scanning that morning, I saw movement. It was 1:34 in the morning. I saw the gate open, and there was Arthur Canden. He just walked to the bench and sat there. When that happened I nearly dropped dead. I knew I had found what had really happened. I could see his mouth move, which showed he was speaking to the fish. He did that occasionally but not often. He wasn't in the right state of mind I had thought! He must be about to kill himself I had thought! But I just sat there watching, expecting. But there was nothing. He did nothing. He just sat there, admiring the fish. I sat there for another 20 minutes, waiting for something to happen on the film. Then finally *something* happened. The gate creaked open, and in came someone. They crept up to Arthur, who I believe fell asleep sometime in those 20 minutes, and they *slowly* stabbed a knife in him! Then they yanked it out and did it immediately again! They did it again! They kept on doing it. There was no sound on the video but I could just hear his blood curdling scream through the pictures."

Dr. Chalice was now looking out the window, anger in her voice; anger at the killer.

"Arthur started running, with all the might he had left. He ran into the light, and the person came after him, into the light, revealing to me that it was none other than Josephine Drew! She ran after him to the gate, and with all of her might chucked her knife at him. He fell on the ground, and rolled over. Even with the grainy feed, I could see him look at her, likely with shock and sorrow, before dying. She dragged him into the pond. She then went back through the gate."

"But, no! I was not done yet. I went and checked the feed, from all of the other cameras. I switched through each of them, following her every footstep. I felt like I was following her in real life! Until I found her at the front entrance, where a pale man stood at the side of a black car with no license plate."

"Josephine Drew was arrested for the muder of Arthur Canden. At the time I could not believe it. I could not see *why!* But as her trial went on, more about her past was revealed. She was found as the murderer of not only Arthur, but *37 other people!* Not only was she a mass murderer, she got away with them too!"

"But let's get back to John DeRusa. That man with the car; he was here the night of the murder," she proceeded to pull out a photo of a black car. "This was outside of the school's entrance."

Inside of the car you could see only one thing; the ghostly figure of a man.

"You see that man in the car? I figured out who he is."

She stopped for dramatic effect.

"That man was the devil himself. He has helped many criminals with murders. He helped Josephine Drew with all of her murders. And, he helped someone murder John. I know your father is the Devil. Now tell me what you know."

CHAPTER 10

What was I supposed to say? She was waiting for me to start talking. Her fingers were crossed and vibrating almost as if she needed to control her anger. Her face had a small smile, proud of her discovery.

I thought about what I was supposed to say. I could tell her about my experience. With the ring, his fiery appearance scarring my mind, ruining my childhood. Instead, I told the lie my mother had told everyone who disapproved of my father's absence. It took all of my little acting experience to lie, as I was not a good one. Using all of the strength I could muster, I started with my alibi.

"Dr. Chalice, even the idea of my father being the devil impales my heart," I started.

Not too slow and not too fast. So far, everything was going great.

"But why not Preston? He is your father after all. You must've seen him somehow. Devils don't look like normal people."

Darn. The questions. I didn't think about what she would say in response. Panicked, I said the first thing to my mind.

"Yes, but do you think, Dr. Chalice, that the Devil would hang around with his kids? He would want to be hidden and in secret. Just like how you explained he did in the murder of John Derusa. Another thing, Dr. Chalice, you accused me by saying that a father would be with me. My father cannot be the devil. My father worked in the harbor for 25 years. He still does. He gets drafted often, and so I don't get to see him much. Never mind the fact that I go to a boarding school."

Immediately, I shut my mouth. Although my words were logically correct, I just had to hope she believed me. She was staring at me for a long time until she got up from her chair and looked out the window.

"Arthur was one of my favorite students, Preston," Dr. Chalice said, her voice cracking like a broken record.

"I know Dr. Chalice."

I worried that I didn't act sympathetic enough.

"And I hope you understand that I will get to the bottom of this no matter what happens. I will tear down whatever stands in my way. Including you," Dr. Chalice said coldly.

She looked back at me, her eyes filled with tears.

"I believe you Preston. A lot of fathers of our students here work at the harbor. Most never come back. You are blessed to have one still alive. You do know that right?" Dr. Chalice asked me.

"Yes Ma'am. And I will do anything in my power to help crack the case," I said, instantly regretting it.

I would have to come up with more lies.

"No Preston. It's better you keep your good grades. While this is happening, it's best we keep the school as normal as possible. Well, that is not regarding the murder." She nodded me off to leave, and I was about to reach the door when she stopped me..

"Preston, may I tell you something?" she asked me with a plea in her eyes.

She looked like a child. I nodded and stepped towards her.

"If you hear anything about Johnny, do tell me please?" she asked me with her hands clasped together.

I nodded and went out the door, rubbing my finger. How long would I be able to lie about this? I immediately stopped rubbing when I saw Elizabeth waiting around the corner.

"You're mighty good at lying," she told me, with a smirk on her face.

"I wonder who I get it from," I said coldly walking in her direction.

She smiled an annoyed and admiring smile, and followed me. Before I went down the stairs I stopped.

"I was too afraid to enter the place where you led me before. Take me back there, now. I'm ready," I said without even realizing.

But I was ready. I could do this. And I needed to know EVERYTHING. But she wasn't moving. Almost trying to see if I was being serious.

"What are you waiting for?" I asked her. "Ladies first."

CHAPTER 11

I once again followed Elizabeth through the winding maze that I had first feared. We arrived at the door, and I looked up at nightmares in front of me, before I took a deep breath. There was no way I was cowering again. Elizabeth stepped to the side and gestured to me, giving me access to the door.

"It's okay, I'm here. And there is no way I'm going to let anything bad happen to you. Plus, if it makes you feel any better. Most things on the other side of that door are either scared, or in favor of me. They can't hurt you," she said. Her voice was calm and collected, but at the same confident, and powerful.

There was nothing I could do but trust it. Even if it was beyond my will. I slowly raised my shaking hand to the cool silver doorknob and turned it. Slowly, and without a sound, it opened up. I pushed past it and walked through. On the other side of the wall, was a huge room. With dark burgundy colored walls and a black quartz floor. There were a few groups of people who turned their heads to look at us, well mostly me. There were also many large and small demonic creatures alike. Elizabeth slipped past me.

"Come," she said simply.

And I did. Our shoes clacked slightly with every contact they made with the floor, and it echoed through the silent room. There were big crystal chandeliers hanging from the ceiling fifty feet above our heads. We passed a couple benches and then finally, sat down in the furthest one back. My mind was racing, begging for a logical explanation for it all, but I could not speak. We were just sitting there in silence, me looking around the peculiar room skeptically, and Elizabeth at nothing in particular.

"Elizabeth!"

My head snapped to my side to see the ugliest thing ever walking up to us. It had the hairy body of a spider, but with a single sharp claw on the end of every foot. With huge bull horns and small red eyes. It was perhaps just a little smaller than me. It's voice was high pitched and slurred. It brushed past me and I gagged as I felt something wet and slimy on its fur. But Elizabeth barely changed her face.

"Oh, it's you," she scrunched her nose. "What do you want?" she asked.

"Nothing, nothing, just wanted to know what brought you back? How long you would be staying and when you expect to leave, you know?" Elizabeth rolled her eyes.

"You know, I could stay. But if I were you I would stop nosing around in everyone's business, most importantly, mine. Especially if you want to keep the remaining relatives you have."

I blinked at the threat. The monster looked us up and down one last time before turning and crawling away to others like her.

"I'm guessing those are the relatives!" Liz scoffed. "Wow, the audacity to come up and talk to me like that. It was like she was asking to be alone," she shook her head and leaned into the bench. I sat up straighter.

"So, what is this place exactly?" I asked her.

"This Preston, is The Lobby," she answered.

"The lobby to what?"

"No, the name of this place is The Lobby. It's where creatures and people alike go if they need an audience, a message sent, or any business whatsoever, with the Devil. Not many people know of it, but if you get involved with the Devil, you're bound to know about it sooner than later."

"So you have business with the devil?" I said.

She turned to look at me.

"You could say. But the real reason you're here is because you said you could keep a secret," she clarified.

"Yes, because you told me you worked for a devil. And then you also told me how you killed John. Does the Devil have anything to do with that?"

"Everything," she told me. "But our ride has arrived, come," and she got up.

We walked to the wall we were by and then to a caged space in it. A small, over-head light blinked white and slid open with a loud scratching of metal sound. She stepped in and as I looked hesitant to it's structural security, but ultimately obliged. And just before it closed behind us, a pale and bony arm stuck itself in between the doors. They pulled the doors apart and entered the elevator of sorts. It was a smaller girl, with a slim figure and short black hair that was dyed pink at the tips. Her porcelain face was detailed with a few freckles.

"I thought I heard your voice, Elizabeth," she said. Elizabeth smiled.

"So you did Maryanne," she smiled and hugged the girl who gladly returned it. Once they pulled away the girl spoke again.

"So what brings you here? Meeting with the man?" She looked at me and gave a sly smile.

"Well, what do we have here? What are you doing bringing a boy to The Lobby? Never seen you bring one."

"No nothing like that. It just so happens that Preston over here has no respect for others' privacy, and got dragged into an assignment of mine. I've come to straighten things out."

"How do you know each other?" I asked before the topic completely changed. Knowing they were girls, it probably would soon. Maryanne answered me.

"We were, umm, interns at a job together. We learned together, we actually shared a room! Good partner, good worker and a good friend," I laughed.

"Good friend? I don't really thinks John would say the same," I stated. Maryanne barely blinked.

"I understand now, well your stop is next. I'll leave you to it."

The doors to the elevator opened and I stepped out. And just as Elizabeth got out, Maryanne grabbed her wrist.

"Lizzie, I know you're extra careful and amazing at what you do. You always were, but be careful. There are rumors floating around like the souls of dead people without their loved ones. As heartless as we both know we are, I do care for you, the boss doesn't. He has no soul, no heart, no care. You know that," she let go of her arm as Liz nodded her head.

"Thank you Mary," she said. Maryanne nodded her head. And as the doors closed, she brought her thumb to her ear and pinky to her mouth.

"Call me!"

I looked at Elizabeth with the word confused written in a bold black letters on my forehead. She waved it off as if it wasn't important. I knew it must have been by the hushed tones Maryanne was using, but there was no use in asking.

We walked down a hallway with dark green wallpaper and a small candle lit every five feet. Passing many doors, we stopped in front of one with the inscription J.D on it and the numbers 107-3 right under. She knocked on the door and from the other side I heard someone say to enter. The room inside had a small white bed, table and other pieces of small furniture and decor. Sitting on his bed, looking much paler and with dark bags under his eyes, was John Derusa. He had a white shirt stained with blood and a pair of gray sweatpants. He noticed me looking at him.

"I can't complain about what I died in. I've seen worse than what I wore to bed that day. If only there was no blood. I would look significantly better."

"I-I'm sorry-"

"It's okay. I know that's not how you meant it."

He looked away from me and to Elizabeth.

"Elizabeth Gray, I'm a bit surprised to see my killer here. You know I understand why you did it. And it's too bad because if I died naturally at this age, I'm gonna bet I would be up in heaven. Heaven instead of freaking hell because one of the Devil's minions killed me."

MY head was spinning at the mention of the Devil's minions. He said Elizabeth was one, just like she had mentioned contacts with a devil. What did everything mean? The killing, why? The reasons, the victim, the killer, it was all for a reason. But for which one? My train of thought was stopped abruptly alongside John and Elizabeth's conversation. Loud thumps were heard and the shaking of chandeliers also. He looked to see the ceiling shaking under whatever pressure was being put on it. I looked back down at Elizabeth quickly, who was sharing a conversation with John. He nodded his head.

"He knows," Elizabeth grabbed my hand and started rushing out as quickly as possible.

"What's wrong?" I yelled at her over all the noise. She turned, making her hair fly behind her.

"We have to get out of here."

CHAPTER 12

"Well. I guess I don't know. Well...," I stand there thinking how I can fix my mistakes. "Ok fine, I grew up knowing that somehow I *was* related to the Devil. And maybe he is my father, maybe not. But I had some connection to him." I make sure not to say everything, but at this time I think I haven't leaked too much.

"What has your mother said about this?"

"Well, I have never specifically asked her about this, but-"

"Well why don't you ask her?"

"I-I haven't spoken to her in years."

"Do you want to know though?"

"I guess." We walk in silence for a while. But I am not going to go visit my mom."

"But yet, maybe you should," she says then scurries away.

"I'm not visiting my mother...," I mutter as I walk to the dorm.

* * *

So what am I doing less than 12 hours later? I am packing my stuff to head down south to go visit my mother. It's a little after 5am, and it is still dark out. There is a little drizzle, but not too much for me to lug an umbrella along for the ride. I leave a note next to Coley and I head out the door, towards Church.

* * *

Church is a really quiet town. It's streets are paved with cobblestone, all cracked of age, and all of the houses in Church are made out of wood. I'm standing at the side of the tracks, hoping that I haven't missed the 5:37 train to London. It is already 5:40.

It is still dark out, and no one is at the station. The Church functions on a completely foreign calendar than I grew up with. The people here don't wake any later than 5, and less than 12 hours later, they're all back asleep. If you can find more than 2 people out after dark, you're lucky. So I was surprised to see no one today. On weekdays, by the time I can go to Church, everything is already closed. So I don't come here often.

Just when I see the clock strike 5:45, the train pulls up. *Thank god it's late.* I lug my heavy backpack onto my back, and step onto the cool train.

I take a seat mid way through the last car. No one else is in this car, which relieves me. I've had some foul experiences with people on trains. As we pull away, I hear the train siren sound.

"Next stop, Greenberg."

The sun starts rising while I'm eating a breakfast granola bar. I'm not really a morning person but I am not tired right now.

The last time I saw my mother was 5 years ago. For most of my life she lived in Denmark. Her father worked for the UN as a representative for the UK, even though he grew up in the US. My mother lived in 7 different countries before she was 10, but they finally settled down in the countryside of Denmark after my Grandfather retired.

When I was 5, my mother met Elliot, my stepfather. We moved to the south of England soon after that. We lived in a little house on a hill in a small town, Varden. Varden is just an hour south of London, right on the border of England and Wales.

When I was 9, I went to Coventry. There was something she wanted to get me away from, but I did not know what.

She visited me every other week for the first few months at Coventry. Gradually, however, she lowered the amount of times she visited until I didn't even see her at all. She still wrote me letters from time to time, but it was as if she wanted to cut me out of her life. But I had always wondered why, so I just kept her out of my head.

I stopped thinking about my past and I got up to stretch my legs which were numb. When I sat back down, I could do nothing to keep my eyes open...

* * *

"Yo Preston."

I jolt awake at the sound of someone saying my name. I turn around, and there is Elizabeth sitting behind me.

"What the heck? How did you get here? Am I dreaming?"

"I saw you leave Coventry and I followed you, but I didn't see which car you went on, so I went onto the first one, and every stop we had, I moved down a car. Why did you have to take the last one?"

"Why are you here?"

"I want to make sure you don't chicken out, that's why."

"I wouldn't have."

We don't talk at all for the rest of the ride. I am a little annoyed that Elizabeth came. This should be a private visit. We arrived in London half past 8. The station is filled to the brim with people, and it takes us 20 minutes alone to get out. Once we do, I hail us a cab.

"37 Handle St, Varden."

"That's far."

"What, you only do local?"

So we ended up walking 10 minutes to a different taxi depot that does hour plus rides. It wasn't that nice of a car. There were cigarette holes all over the back seat, and the window didn't work.

At 10 o'clock, we were there. I saw the vine covered house. The one that I called home most of my life. The mailbox was still askew. The attic still had a window cover for no window.

You could say I was home.

I walked up the concrete steps, and knocked on the door with the gargoyle knocker. I heard creaking inside, and then fiddling with the doorknob.

I then see my mother. She looks at me in surprise.

"Oh Preston hello!" she gives me a quick hug, before she ushers me inside. She closes the door before Elizabeth could come in.

"It's fair to say I was not expecting a visit," she says, nervously.

I think of what to say. It is just so awkward now that it has been so long. I sit on the brown rocking chair in the family room as my mother goes to the kitchen to turn off the stove.

When she returns, she gives me a plate of saltine crackers.

"So Preston, how is Coventry?"

"It's alright," I answer.

"Why did you not send me a letter that you were finally visiting?"

"It was sort of a momentary decision," I said. I was about to ask her when she interrupts.

"You look awfully pale, are you ok Preston?"

"Yeah I am fine," I answer and she gives me a blanket. The room *is* chilly. But I shouldn't let this drag on in my head. I should cut to the chase.

"Mother, I must ask you something, and it may come as a surprise, or it may not. But, here it is," I pause for a moment, contemplating whether I really should ask. *Do I want to know?* "Is my father the Devil?"

CHAPTER 13

Preston ascended the worn wooden steps with trepidation, eyeing the doorbell as though it was a coiled adder, taut and poised to strike. As he cautiously extended his hand, images, sounds, emotions flashed across his mind, hazy yet unmistakably real. His mother, holding him, rocking, humming a lullaby. Him leaning against her in exhaustion as they returned from a long walk outside. That house, with it's pale blue curtains and uneven shingles, i'ts tiny herb garden and tree with a swing hanging from it, swaying in the brisk autumn breeze. How long had it been, since he had sat in that seat, the wind flying through his hair, without a care in the world but there and then? How many years since he had been a perfectly ordinary toddler, enjoying his perfectly ordinary life? Ten? Twelve? Time unbound?

He thought of his childhood, growing up in that house, and how he had spent his younger days frolicking in the fields that surrounded the abandoned manor just outside of town, exploring where others his age would not have dared, among endless carpeted hallways and salons, the dust thick in the air. The thought of the last time he had been there, the vague dread that accompanied blankness when he tried to recall why he had, for years since, avoided the town like the plague.

A dam broke in his mind, as the steady trickle of memory became a deluge, inundating him with snippets of time, places, things.

A bureau in the manor house, in which he had hid. Cold pale eyes, shining in the light of the moon. A feeling of cold, of abandonment, of utter silence. Two rings set in black velvet. A young girl, a silver knife in her hands. The Devil. His presence was everywhere, everything. What had Challice said? *"'I know your father is the Devil. Now tell me what you know.'"* Well, what did he know? About any of this? Devils and murderers and -

"Preston?"

The doorbell, which he did not recall touching, rang loudly, startling him from his reverie. He looked down to see his hand pressed against it, the tip of his finger turning white with the pressure.

"Coming, coming," murmured a voice from inside.

The door swung open. A woman stood on the threshold, looking slightly aggravated. Her mousy brown hair, silvery at the temples, sat in a mop upon her head. Wide hazel eyes locked on Preston and froze.

"Hello, mother," she said

"Preston?"

My mother looked grave. "We have a lot to talk about," she said.

* * *

Elizabeth trailed behind, lingering uncertainty in the doorway while Preston and his mother walked on. The kitchen-dining-room, with its high bar stools and framed pictures on the walls, brought back memories of the happiest years of his life.

"Do you want some tea? Water? Anything?" his mother asked, retrieving two chipped mugs from the bottom drawer of a tall cabinet against the wall. On top of it sat an ornament, a red glass robin, rendered in detail down to its beady black-painted eyes.

"Yes, that would be great, thanks," I answered.

As the kettle boiled and popped on the stove, Preston sat down at the small circular table. He tried to appear calm as his mother, who he had not seen for years, added bags to the teapot with her back to him, while inside he was a flurry of conflicting emotions: longing and repulsion, fear and anger, unbridled joy and crushing misery.

He registered a mug being set in front of him, his mother sliding onto the stool opposite him. Clearing her throat, she said, slightly awkwardly:

"So, how has Coventry been?"

"Well, other than the murder, just wonderful," I answered sarcastically.

"I heard. Nasty business. Must have been a great shock," she said.

"Indeed," I said.

Preston did not like the knowing look in her eyes as she appraised him.

"The poor parents. And to think that, after all this time..." She trailed off. "Oh, Preston, I've been so worried about you."

"Apparently not enough to come and visit me," I said.

She hung her head.

"Mother, I need to ask you something," I paused. The room seemed to grow colder, a chill settling in the air despite the closed windows.

"Is my father the Devil?"

Preston's mother froze mid-sip, eyes narrowing.

"How - Where did you hear that?"

"Well, is it true?"

She sighed. "You deserve to know the truth. After all these years, that's the least I owe you," she said.

"I'm listening," I waited expectently.

"Very well. It began many years ago, when I had just moved into the village. No, well, even before that, I suppose. When I was young, but a toddler, I dreamed of the Devil. As I lay in my crib one night, humming quietly the tune of the song my mother always sang to me before bed, I realized that I was not alone. I didn't know how he arrived, but there he was: a man, tall and beautiful, his luminous eyes glowing like fragments of far-off stars, brighter than those beyond the wide-open window with its fluttering curtains. As he looked down at me, there was hope in his eyes, and beneath it, crushing sadness. He seemed to drift soundlessly over the wooden boards, his feet never touching the ground. As he reached me, he looked so miserable, so forlorn.

"Our hour is not yet here. One day, we will meet," he said.

"My own heart wept, and I, swaddled in my blankets, wished to wipe his shining tears. I knew him, somehow. I longed to comfort him, to tell him that it was alright, that he would be safe. I reached out a little hand," she continued. Her hazel eyes had taken on a dreamy quality, glassy in remembrance of things better left unthought of, unspoken.

"Cautiously, his eyes never leaving my own, he lay down beside me. I clung to him, desperate to assuage his grief. His embrace was cold but gentle, like ice beneath velvet. I remember that feeling to this day. I began to cry as well, so moved by this man's mysterious anguish. He gave me a gentle squeeze; "I'll miss you, my dear. You are my world, my all, my savior." As I breathed in the faint scent of smoke upon his black suit - so odd, that he already seemed to be mourning - I felt something drip onto my forehead, burning, viscous, and sulphuric. I looked up. Thick black and gold streaked down the cheeks of the face, transformed in an instant into something tarry and monstrous. Horns erupted from his long black hair. His mouth gaped, revealing narrow teeth like a fish. His eyes, suddenly large, were filled with fiery stars. His arms, too many too count, had turned into a prison, tendrils curling around my tiny arms. As they closed around me, I cried out for help - and woke, screaming, no sign of the man's tears upon me, only an indentation in the bed leaving a clue that he had been there at all,"she said almost dreamily.

"Years later, I was living here, in this house, fresh out of school and with hardly a memory of the man I had tried so hard to forget. One night, he appeared on my doorstep, unconscious, torn and broken, but in the same black suit in which he had appeared in what I thought, at the time, to be a dream. I, with the help of my friend Jonothan, took him in and nursed him back to health. When he finally began to recover, he claimed amnesia; he said that all he remembered was his name, Nar Echo, among a few select moments before hitting his head upon my threshold, which he would not divulge, despite my prodding."

"We sent out letters, trying to find where he might have come from. All the while he stayed with me, sleeping on my sofa. As time went on, he grew... strange. He became vivacious, flirtatious, desperate to maintain my attention. He would hardly let me out of his sight, growing nervous when I left each morning for work, positively furious after long nights at the clinic. Despite this oddness and the childhood vision that was so difficult to escape, I still cherished his presence. Though he had an inexplicable dislike for Jonothan, I began to feel something for this apparent stranger. One night, around a year after he had first come to stay with me, when we were alone in this very house, he professed his love to me. I returned his affection, and one thing led to another...

"The next day, I considered telling Jonothan everything, but could not get the words out when he proposed to me that evening."

She looked so miserable, as she sat there on the bar stool.

"I continued like this for a month or so. I don't know what I thought could happen, living my two lives, but I didn't have the courage to tell either of them. I wish I had."

"I became pregnant. I didn't know who the father was, but when "Nar" found out, he was furious. He flew into a rage, and I didn't see him again for days. The morning after he left, Jonothan disappeared and, like the fool I was, I thought that he had left me, as well.

"When "Nar" returned, he apologized for his behavior, and asked me if I still loved him. Heartbroken as I was over Jonothan, I couldn't help but say yes. We were married within the year, and then I had you.

"For years after, he came and went. He said that he was away on business for his new job, but I never knew what he was really up to, at the time. Whenever he saw you, he seemed filled with the same kind of loathing that he had fixated upon poor Jonothan. And there were other things, eating away at me; Jonothan's friends, who knew nothing of his apparent flight, began to search for him. The whole time, you grew older, happy and blissfully unaware of what was happening around you."

"He started acting even more bizarrely, as people came in and out of the house and he sequestered himself in his ever-locked office, and I was so afraid, Preston. I began to put two and two together. The more I tried to learn about this man, the further I dug into his mysterious associates, the more terrified I became."

"And then the remains of Jonothan's body were found in a ditch outside town, slashed by what seemed to be massive claws. I confronted my husband, showed him the evidence I had gathered. I told him that I knew what he had done to John, what he had done to countless others.

That he was the Devil. The monster that I knew had lurked just beneath the surface made its appearance, and he left me for dead, bleeding out on this floor. He took you up to the old ruins, and I never saw you again, until today."

The sun filtering through the window turned the robin momentarily bright, aflame, an angelic phoenix burning, burning and falling out of the sky. As my mother's tears plunked on the wood of the table, I felt a chill settle in the air.

CHAPTER 14

Preston meticulously wiped the sweat from his forehead. His shirt was now soaked in sweat so wiping the sweat didn't do much but it calmed him nonetheless. His brain was still foggy from what he heard inside just a few moments ago. He attempted furiously to understand what his mother had told him. He just couldn't understand why he had to be the son of the Devil. Why he had to be cursed and have the rest of his life ruined and masked by blood, fire and whatever else came with being the Devil's son. The more he thought about the curse, his father and his mother his breathing became more rushed and labored. He opened his eyes, halting his ludicrousy.When Preston looked up he was surprised to see Elizabeth walking out of his house with a container full of cookies and having a nice chat with his mother. The door shut and Elizabeth came towards him as his mother went back inside without so much as a glance to Preston. Elizabeth gave Preston a sympathetic smile as she walked by him softly saying,

"We should probably head back towards Coventry Gardens now."

Preston followed thoughtfully, still scared, angry and confused about what he had heard. Preston had thought that Elizabeth would want nothing to do with him, especially with him being the Devil's son, but now as he thought about the fact that she was a murderer, he realized that nothing must faze her. He sullenly followed her in silence walking across the endless valley of green ahead of them. They were headed back into the woods a few miles out from Coventry Gardens before either of them spoke a word.

"Do you want to talk about what just happened?" Elizabeth asked.

"I just don't understand how you aren't scared of me or running away or even just killing me like the murderer you are," Preston said.

Elizabeth seemed hurt for a moment but then understanding how Preston felt, ignored his comment.

"You know I didn't choose to be a murderer you know," she said.

Preston chuckled under his breath. "As if it was a choice" he muttered.

"You're right, it was not a choice," she said.

Preston rolled his eyes and suddenly Elizabeth became worried and began in a panicked tone to tell Preston "Preston, you need to listen to me. You being the Devil's son is really not our problem here and I need you to listen to me for a second," she said urgently.

Preston's hands suddenly began shaking and all of his thoughts and emotions from the past few hours came crashing down at once. Preston rushed away from Elizabeth, away from anything alive, anything that could see him in this state. He found a tree deep in the woods and began to climb. It came naturally to him finding branch after branch, calculating each step making sure he couldn't fall.

Eventually he reached the top of a near 50 foot tree. He could see the whole woods from above and silently lay watching the sun disappearing over a mountain in the distance. The sights calmed him. He began to slow his breathing letting himself drift away beginning to now truly think about what his mother had just told him. He had already known about his father somewhat, but to hear that he had been cursed, scared him to death. What could the curse be? Could he never be happy or was he sentenced to a life in hell. Whatever it was he knew it would never be safe for him to go back to Coventry Gardens.

He lay for a moment letting silence enter his mind as a soft drizzle began to sting the ends of his hair. The drizzle soon became a bit more of a rain and Preston resorted to climbing down about 20 feet from where he then was able to see Elizabeth tired and out of breath, hollering at him. He ignored her not wanting anything to do with the world below him and intending to keep it that way for as long as possible. Soon Elizabeth stopped yelling and tried to coax him down as if he was a dog begging for food at the table. He scoffed, shocked that she thought it would be so easy to get him to leave his perch in the trees.

The rain was beginning to fall harder now and Preston was going to have to leave the tree and reach common ground with the earth again. Savoring every last moment up on the tree Preston began to slowly work his way down the limbs of the tree. Elizabeth relaxed on the ground, relieved that Preston was finally coming down. Preston neared the ground and could see Elizabeth looking at him. She had a sad smile on her face. Preston jumped the last five feet down from the tree landing with a grunt. Elizabeth began to speak immediately, "Preston I know how you feel," she said. He looked up but ignored her.

"Please listen to me, I have been honest with you before, why not trust me now, one more time, see what happens?" He glared at her.

"Why should I trust a murderer?"

"I tried to tell you before, I never chose to become a murderer, I was forced to," Elizabeth said.

"How can you be forced to be a murderer?"

"Preston you're not the only one with a connection to the devil!"

The pain seared through Preston's body. It began the moment Elizabeth's hand made a connection with his. The ground around him was fading and Preston's eyes were going blurry. Fighting through the pain he managed to wave his hand before his eyes and as he did he nearly passed out at the sight of his ring finger. It was as if all the veins in his body had pushed the blood from his heart to his finger and then burst. He looked over at Elizabeth who was also on the ground yelling and screaming in agony. Preston looked back at his hand which now looked as if it had been mauled by the air. He saw a golden glint poking through the side of his finger.

A memory flashed before his eyes of a ring being placed around his finger and then vanishing deep beneath the depths of his skin. "This must be the curse," he thought." The ring contains the curse." " But that doesn't make sense, Elizabeth is on the ground too." Thoughts began ringing through his mind racing around a track. Preston became so lost in his thoughts he didn't realize that the burning in his hand had stopped. He opened his eyes now realizing that the pain had ceased. He took in the sight around him.

There was blood dripping from his hand and the ground was coated with a red layering. He looked around for Elizabeth but he didn't see her anywhere. He did see the blood covering the many branches she had fallen upon, but still no Elizabeth. He began yelling her name as loud as he could. He couldn't care less if the Devil heard him and came after him. Then he remembered Elizabeth had been saying he was not the only one with a connection to the Devil. Could she mean herself or did she mean someone else? It was unclear to him, but he did have an underlying panicky thought. If Elizabeth really did have a connection to the Devil like Preston then maybe, maybe the Devil has taken her. Taken her because of whatever just happened when their hands connected. What if she was being tortured, even killed. Then Preston realized he had forgotten about his hand.

CHAPTER 15

I heard the sound of twigs breaking as the person walked over to me. Their pace got faster and faster with every step until they reached me. I heard the person sigh in relief.

"Thank god you're okay," and lowered the lamp to reveal themself. It was Coley. I sighed in relief also.

"It's you," I said. Coley looked at me.

"Well duh! Who else did you think I was?" he asked me. "A murderer,? Elizabeth?

some weird creature? You never know these days.

"Nobody," I replied. I could tell he didn't believe me.

"Well c'mon then, it's dark out," he said. He walked up beside me and put his arm under mine to support me. My injuries were minor, and my hand was still full of blood and wearing a golden ring.

Under and over branches, logs and rocks, the school was getting easier and easier to see. I realized that it was the first time I had ever seen Coley walk through the forest. How did he know exactly where we were going? And how did he know where to find me?

"Coley?" I asked.

"Yes Preston?" he replied to me.

"How did you know where to find me?" he slowed down our pace as I asked him the question. He didn't answer for a minute, trying to figure out what the best way to respond would be.

"Preston, we have to get you to the dorm, you can ask me stuff there when you are cleaned up and warm," I nodded my head.

As soon as we entered our dorm, unnoticed, Coley dragged me to the bathroom. He told me to take a shower and then he left. I did as he asked and then went back to my room. On my bed was a sweatshirt and sweatpants. I saw Coley put away some homework out of the corner of my eye, as I sat down on my bed. Coley got up and sat down at the end of mine.

"You know, you were one of the first friends I made, right," he told me.

"Ya," I replied.

"You're the only reason I have more nowadays, if I hadn't become friends with you at the beginning, I wouldn't have any more now. I was the loner kid in the back of the class. In every single school, it was always the same. And you're the reason that all changed," Coley said sincerely.

"Coley, if you were the kid that never spoke to anyone, why did you come up to me?"

"Preston, I got to this school, looked around at all the kids and saw that you were like me. In the back of the class. You never talked to anyone. And then obviously our dorm situation helped with me talking to you too," he chuckled silently. "You helped me conquer a fear of mine. Thank you" it was my turn to smile.

"Coley, I need to tell you something. But you have to swear on your life you won't tell anyone," I told him. He put his hand on his heart.

"I promise," he said. I took a deep breath.

"My father's the devil."

"I know." My head snapped up in his direction. His facial expression had not changed a bit.

"H-how did you know?" I asked in a stutter.

"Preston I'm not only your friend. I was sent here to protect you,` `he admits.

"Protect me! From what?" I asked as I got up. He rolled his eyes.

"Protect you from what?! I found you in the forest injured and with your hand covered full of blood. You are also the Devil's son, anything could go wrong with that title. And I mean someone in our school was murdered less than a week ago. Protect you from what?! I seriously think you hit your head," he sounded off. More and more annoyed as he went on, so I stopped him.

"If you knew, why did you not tell me?"

"It wasn't in my place to tell you. Plus if I had told you, you never would have gone to see your mother. How is she by the way? I haven't seen her in years," he asked me. I shook my head.

"You know my mother," I said.

"Yup. I mean we needed permission to have a protector with you," he told me.

"What's with everyone being friends with my mom? First, you met her years ago and just asked me how she is, and Elizabeth got a container full of cookies from her! And who is 'We'?" I spoke, my voice getting more and more confused.

"'We' Is the organization I'm with. You've been to The Lobby if I'm correct?" I nodded.

"And so you know that it's full of monsters, people who have business with your father, the Devil. I'm with a group of people against him. Were the opposite really. Trying to do good. Not bad, like your father. No offense," he said to me.

"None taken," I assured him.

"The Gateway, that's where the organization I'm part of goes, and we have been at war with The Lobby for centuries. But being at war means we spy on each other. We have people working undercover in The Lobby. And because of that, we know some people who work for the Devil. Not all of them, but a few. We also got information that someone from The Lobby is responsible for killing John. We don't know who exactly, or why. But it is still important information."

I hung my head down slightly. What would they do to Elizabeth if they discovered it was her? What would I do? I wouldn't be able to let her go easily. I do love her, there was no doubt about that. But she was a murderer, and she must have some relation to the Devil. Especially since she knows about The Lobby.

"So you're telling me that you're part of an organization that is against the Devil's and that you're here to protect me. And that both clans, groups, whatever they are, are in the middle of a war? And you all think someone is going to kill again, maybe me. And you knew that my father was the Devil and DIDN'T TELL ME ANYTHING!" I yelled the last part.

Coley nodded every time I said a fact.

"Yup that's pretty much the gist of it," he said to me.

I sat down on the floor quickly. It hurt but I was in stage one of shock. So at this point, not much could really affect me. That was until I reached the point where everything would finally get inside my brain and I would go crazy. I have learned way too much in the past twenty-four hours. And then suddenly, there was a knock at the door. I slowly turned my head in the direction of the noise in annoyance. What was next? Did someone else die?! Coley got up to answer but after a second they opened it on their own. And I stood up as I saw who was there.

It was Maryanne. She and Coley were staring each other down in disgust.

"What are you doing here, Devil spawn?" he questioned her.

"That's not really any of your business now," she replied. She turned to me. "Your father would like a word with you." I gulped and turned to look at Coley. This was worse than someone dying.

CHAPTER 16

"Hurry now," Maryanne spoke while her feet glided across the grass carrying her feet ahead of Preston and Coley.

Preston gulped as he realized where they were heading. It was the direction of the pond. The pond that Dr. Chalice had shown him in the video of the now murdered boy. Coley stiffly moved past Preston who was taking a moment to catch himself and begin to find the calm mindset he would need for the excursion with his father. Maryanne was at the edge of the pond before she turned around to see Coley and Preston standing, staring off into the distance. What Maryanne was missing from her angle was a horrifying sight.

Elizabeth was sprinting towards Preston and Coley from far off in the woods, blood spewing from her shirt, tears streaming from her eyes and a dagger in hand. Maryanne began to walk towards the boys ready to scold them beneath the earth, but then she saw Elizabeth. Maryanne knew what the boys didn't but the Devil needed Preston for now and she had to stop Elizabeth otherwise things could end disastrously for her, the Devil and most definitely Elizabeth. Maryanne sprinted towards Elizabeth taking her dagger out from behind her as they ran directly at each other. When Maryanne closed the distance between her and Elizabeth to 20 feet she plunged her dagger to the ground, emitting fire and light to erupt the air and ground surrounding Elizabeth.

Preston yelled, "What are you doing to her?" He ran to the fire with a waxed expression across his face. Before he could get near the wall however, Maryanne scooped him into her arms and began sprinting across back to the pond. Coley trailed behind, unable to match the pace of Maryanne but desperate to get to Preston. Desperate to save him. Desperate to take the opportunity to have a chance to do what he had set out to do years ago. Desperate to kill the Devil.

Preston screeched as Maryanne carried him toward the gate. The gate with the ominous black sedan with the Devil hidden beneath the tinted windows. As they approached, a tall man with stretched skin and dark straight hair stepped out of the car. The man halted for a moment, as if surprised to see Preston, perhaps even angry to see him. Despite this as Preston and Maryanne approached, he lightened his blank face and put an evil smile over his clawlike teeth. Preston had halted his screaming the second that the Devil had been in sight. He couldn't let the Devil see any signs of weakness or fear. Maryanne put Preston down once they had passed the gate entrance and then the gate shut with a clang.

"NO!" Preston shouted.

Coley, who had been left behind when Maryanne had picked Preston up, was now locked inside the woods. Maryanne hit Preston over the head, shutting him up immediately.

"Marryanne," the Devil croaked.

His voice was harder than a rock. Hard enough to put an itch in Prestons throat the second he heard it. Maryanne walked over to the Devil and they began to whisper. Preston itched to hear what they were speaking of ,but he knew that he had to play smart, for the next few minutes at least. Suddenly, the rocky voice of the Devil came to Preston's ears, not because Preston was closer to him, but more of the fact that the Devil was beginning to yell.

"Even if you don't know the plan, you have to assume that anyone involved with me is doing what I told them to do. This was MY CHANCE. MY ONLY CHANCE. I may never have another opportunity like this to finish the only chance of my demise."

"I am sorry." Maryanne responded.

"Sorry won't do here, you can never repay the mistake you have made."

There was a soft noise, something of a fly buzzing around and then a panicked cry from Maryanne.

"Please, I will never make another mistake, you know I am forever devoted."

The devil laughed and then there was a soft thud and Maryanne was shrieking. Preston, who had withdrawn from peeking over at the Devil at this point turned his head, unable to process what could possibly be going. When Preston looked ove,r the sight before him was something he thought he would never see in his entire life. The Devil, who was now turning back towards his sedan, was standing over Maryanne, or what used to be Maryanne. The was a dagger much like the one Elizabeth and Maryanne had carried, sticking out of Maryannes chest. The dagger wasn't just killing Maryanne but it was also burning her. The dagger, brightly lit with fire, was emitting itself across every point of Maryannes body it could find, eventually covering her entirely.

Two doors of the sedan opened and then there were two men, identical in black suits and white gloves. The men moved over towards Maryanne, they removed the dagger, halting the flames, picked her up and carried hernto the back of the sedan and placed her in the trunk.

"Preston," the Devil called. Preston looked towards him and began to stand up and walk to him. "Please, have a seat," he said, pointing to the car and the open door.

Preston, with his shoes sticky and wet with blood slowly, took a seat next to the Devil who had almost gleefully jumped into the sedan just before him.

"Now Preston, you may be wondering why I have called you here," the Devil insured.

"Why yes, most definitely," Preston answered, keeping his answer tart and not giving the Devil the pleasure of knowing that the sight of Maryanne may have disturbed him in any way.

"Well, let me tell you. I have called you here today because I would like to speak to you about who you should trust, and who you should ignore," said the Devil softly putting his finger to his lips as Preston nearly interrupted him.

"Yes, I know who you have been speaking to about the murder of John Deruso and I know what you have told and been told. I need you to understand that you can by no means listen to Dr. Chalice. As for Coley and Elizabeth you should be okay there but I want to make sure that you are very careful with Dr. Chalice. She has been unsuccessfully prosecuting me for years."

There was a hush through the car, the only noise leaking through was the humming of the engine. "You have to trust me Preston. I know what is best for you. I am your father." Preston stopped breathing. He had known that this man was his father but the fact that he had openly said that he was Preston's father caught him off guard.

"Yes my dear boy. I am your father and I am trying to save you."

"Are you the Devil?" Preston asked.

"My son, yes. I am indeed the devil."

CHAPTER 17

I wake to the sound of sirens outside my window. I have a pounding headache, and my eyes are sore. I swerve to my side and see the clock read 5:15. I then roll back and stuff a pillow to each of my ears. I attempt to drown out the noise, but eventually, I succumb to the sirens, and give up on my attempt to sleep again.

As I get up, I notice that Coley is nowhere to be seen. Ever since John DeRusa was killed he'd been acting strangely. I didn't know if that was really the reason but that was the best explanation I could offer.

His confession of his organization yesterday really caught me off guard, and frankly, I don't actually know how much I believe that. Sure, he knew Maryanne, but that could be attributed to other things. Maybe. He actually hasn't seemed the same for a couple of months. He kept himself more hidden from me, but I assumed he should know everything about me. *How have I not noticed this until now?*

I hit my head just hard enough to stop my train of thought. I went over to the window and opened up the shade to see a swarm of fire trucks, police cars, and a couple of unmarked military vans. *What the heck?*

I grab a granola bar and leave the dorm to further investigate. Instead of going out the front, I went through the back exit so I could avoid the cops for now.

"Psst. Preston," whispers someone sharply from the bushes near the parking lot. "Preston."

I look over to see Elizabeth hiding behind a large bush. As I walk over, I can see her face is terrified.

"Come here," she whispers."Why are all those cops there? And why are you hiding?"

"They've come to arrest me!" she says louder than intended.

"What?"

"I am pretty sure they are here to arrest me!"

"What do they know??"

She hesitated for a second, "I heard them mention John," she says in a barely audible whisper. "They know."

No, oh no. "Are you sure they know?" I say that almost more to myself than to Elizabeth. "I can go and see what they do know. Yeah I'll go do that." I get up, and right when I start walking, she calls me back.

"Preston, wait."

I stopped, but now I too was curious. "But-"

"Preston. I need to run away."

I was starstruck. A bombshell just fell. "Are you sure they know? I-"

"Yes. I need to run away. And..." she paused for a moment thinking. "And I need you to come with me."

"But shouldn't I go check first?"

"You're not taking this seriously enough!" she stopped, hurt at the way I had been acting. But, to my defense, it *was* 5 in the morning.

"Preston. That's not all I need to run from."

"What do you mean?"

"I mean...I need to run from the Devil."

"What is he going to do to you?"

"Not me. Preston, *you're* my next assignment."

CHAPTER 18

Oh my gosh. Oh my gosh. Breathe Preston breathe. I was shaking the way animals do after they escape their predators. *Is Elizabeth actually going to kill me? I can't go with her.*

I looked at Elizabeth. The plea filled her eyes, begging me to go with her. I shook my head. First very slowly, seeing what her reaction would be. In her response, she put her hand on my arm, which I shook off. Slowly I became more confident. She whimpered, and covered her face with her arms.

"Elizabeth. I love you." She looked up at me with tears in her eyes making her even more beautiful than before. "I want to keep you safe from the authorities, and Dr. Chalice, and the police. If I could, I would hide you in my backpack and fight to the death to be with you. But when you tell me that your next assignment is to kill me? I can't Elizabeth, I can't." When I finished, I took a deep breath thinking about what I did.

Before I knew it, I did something unimaginable. I wrapped my arms around her and gave her a kiss. It was something that I had wanted to do for the longest time, and something that I could only do now. At first her breath tastes like peppermint, and those blueberry scones from breakfast. But soon, it tasted fiery, and I could feel her longing to kill me. After what the Devil had done to her, and to us, she couldn't control it. I quickly let go to see her face red as a beet. Whether it was that she enjoyed the kiss or wanted to kill me, I didn't know.

Before I could really think about it, I sprinted back to the dorm room. Back to safety. Back to Coley. I didn't stop running until I reached our dorm. When I slammed the door Coley was there waiting for me. Tired, I hugged him, and told him everything.

"I figured, the Devil would send her to you at some point," he said, making a jerking movement with his hand when something shiny caught my eye.

A butcher knife. My best friend had a butcher knife in his pocket. His small frame looked larger holding the knife. He looked... powerful. He stormed out the door before I could question what he was doing. I ran after him, knowing that there was only one thing he could do with that shimmering knife.

"COLEY!" I yelled, panting. "Coley, wait up! You can't kill her!" I said. He whipped around a knife pointed at me accusingly.

"Why Preston? So that you could save your little girlfriend? If I don't kill her, you die. I am not gonna let that happen," he yelled. Sprinting he ran towards the elevator slamming the button that closed the elevator faster. When I reached the elevator, he was long gone. Being on the 10th floor of Coventry Gardens was sometimes convenient. Now, it was absolutely dreadful. There was only one elevator which meant I had to take the stairs. Groaning, I sprinted down the long circular staircase that was used as fire exits. When I finally reached the bottom, Coley was already with Elizabeth.

"If you just gave in this would be so much easier," Coley said hate rimming his voice.

"It's not that easy, Coley," Elizabeth responded.

"You could make it easy. But you think you are so deceitful. You think you can charm me with your words and your voice. But trust me Elizabeth there is nothing in this world that would make me enjoy any moment with you. Besides, you dare try and take Preston away? So that you could kill him? So that you can keep it a secret and do all of the Devil's bidding? I don't think so."

"I don't want to kill him, Coley," she responded.

"You managed to kill John. You didn't want to do that either. And yet, Elizabeth and yet, you did it anyway," Coley responded.

"The Devil threatened me."

"You're lying to me."

"I'm not, Coley."

"You think I'm stupid? I know what happened all the way from the beginning. I saw you help put the ring on Preston. So now, to put things right, I am going to kill you." He ran towards her, knife glimmering in the sun, and I knew I had to do something. Running as fast as my legs could take me, which was surprisingly fast, I pushed Elizabeth aside, knocking her to the ground.

"You're an idiot Elizabeth. I am going to kill you. He started to charge again, but using all of my energy I pulled him away.

"No, Coley. Don't kill her," I begged. He scrambled trying to get away from me, but hearing my voice, stopped struggling.

"Thank you Preston. Now you can come with me. We are wasting time. See what he has done to you? Now Coley is more of a threat than I am. Let's go," Elizabeth said, starting to back away. I almost started to follow her when Coley stopped me short.

"Preston. Don't you dare follow her. I would never do anything to hurt you."

For a split second I could see the guilt in his eyes. Wanting to cry about everything, wanting to be scared. But he was keeping a poker face. For me. For my sake. To protect my life.

"Preston. Remember what you said? You said you loved me? Remember that Preston?" Elizabeth said, now knowing that Coley would not give up without a fight. Coley cocked his head looking at me.

"YOU SAID THAT TO HER?!" he bellowed with a voice I never knew he had inside of him.

"I'm sorry, Coley! I just... I always wanted to say that to her."

"And you thought that the time she told you she was going to kill you was the right time?"

"No. I mean yes, but I shouldn't have, ok Coley?" I said, honestly afraid of him.

"Oh so now you take it back? Preston, you kissed me! For five minutes!" she said accuslinginly, hurt lining her voice.

"PRESTON!!!! What is wrong with you?"

"I didn't know it was five minutes, I'm sorry. I really like you Elizabeth, I want to protect you... Coley, you're my best friend," I said, shaking.

"Well you've got us in a sticky situation then huh Preston?"

CHAPTER 19

"I'm so sorry, Preston. It's for your own good."

Coley burst forward in a blur of motion, toward Elizabeth, knife in hand, eyes savage with rage, the edges of his mouth curved upwards in a sneer.

The world seemed to slow. Coley's legs moved as though through water. Elizabeth's eyes widened in surprise. Preston tried to move, to do something, finding his legs stricken with the same near-paralysis. Awash in the bloody aura of the rising sun, the grass a million murderous blades, the lawn seemed to radiate a dull, apocalyptic glow. Time stretched in the early morning quiet. From far away came the wailing of a siren.

The trance broke. Elizabeth's hand shot out, her eyes snapping shut in resignation. Coley's course didn't waver, arms pumping, knife shining.

He stopped in his tracks as though he had hit some invisible wall. For a moment, he just stood there, swaying slightly. Coley looked down for a moment at his chest, blinked once, and dropped with a muffled thud on the morning dew.

He landed face up. Emerging from his chest was the hilt of a knife, just long enough so that its glittering tip poked through his flannel shirt.

Behind him stood Elizabeth. A blank expression had settled on her face, and her hand was empty.

Coley was dead. And she had killed him.

CHAPTER 20

There is gray. Only gray. No clouds, no trees. Just gray. Just me in a gray room with my best friend's body lying beneath me. The gray walls turn like clocks. Spinning round and round waiting till I snap. Waiting for me to realize that this is no dream, that this body in front of me is real, that I can't escape the realities. A door is sitting directly across from me, nearly invisible in the surrounding gray. Closing my eyes I stepped over Coley. His blood was paving a path through the never ending gray, leading me to the door. A handle jutted out from the door as I approached. It was golden. It was as if the room was congratulating me for escaping its horrors. As I turn the handle the smell of fresh murder and an endless burning flame reach my nose again. The gray walls dissipate into the soil by my feet and the golden handle I had held just a moment ago has now evaporated.

Looking around I see that I am still in this grassy knoll by the pond. Where just a moment ago Elizabeth had murdered Coley. I slowly turn towards where Coley's body should be lying. His body is gone. No body, but blood. As much as I wish I might have been hallucinating I know it is in no way a possibility. A fierce rage builds slowly inside me the more I process the situation. Elizabeth, Elizabeth murdered Coley. She didn't hesitate. She killed him an instant, before he even had a chance to fight back. It was what I had overlooked about Elizabeth this whole time. Elizabeth worked for the Devil and the Devil only. She didn't care about the life of Coley. She didn't care about my life. She only cares for the Devil. I yell. An erratic strangled scream. That's all I can do to not cry. I think of looking for Elizabeth to see if she may have possibly stayed around to pay for her actions. For her to feel what she had done to Coley. To know what it's like to be betrayed. As I knew it would be, the small search was useless. Only igniting the rage inside me. Where do I go now? I have no home. Coventry Gardens is spewing with murderers and my mother, well my mother is not an option.

"Preston," a voice says from behind me.

I pull the dagger he had pulled from the ground where Coley's body should be lying at this moment, ready and willing to kill whoever hides behind the voice. I relax my arm as I see Maryanne.

"Elizabeth, she killed Coley," I say, choking on the words.

She nods. A simple gesture with so much meaning. As if she is apologizing for the death. As if there was nothing that could have been done. Despite the fact that I could have stopped Coley. Could have done anything, could have sacrificed myself to save Coley. But no. I did none of this.

I stood there, a man sitting and watching a silent black and white film from afar.

"Preston we have to go back to the gateway," Mary-anne spoke tentatively.

I nodded and walked past her in silence. We walk through the beautiful iridescent waters surrounding the pathway of the Gateway in utter silence. Each step through the water a punch in the face. Each step still taken by me, another is taken from Coley. Each step another that could have been his. Maryanne stops before the gate to the Gateway.

"You and I both know Elizabeth well. We both thought we knew that she could become a better person. We both thought that this could all have been avoided," as she took a sharp inhale.

"I think we both know what has to happen now."

CHAPTER 21

I ran through the forest until I came upon the back of the entrance. I scanned my card and then I lifted the pothole. I then climbed down the rusty stairs. This was the emergency entrance to the Lobby, and I had only used it once before. I got to the bottom of the stairs and walked through the rusty door. When I came through, I noticed I was at the back end of the entrance. As I walked out backwards, I saw the door for the first time. It was odd how I had never acknowledged it before.

I walked down the long hallways in hope of running into Maryanne, but I couldn't find her anywhere. So instead, I sat down in the lobby, of the lobby, and started reading a magazine.

I was still nervously shaking, and as I sat, I realized something. I realized that I had killed Coley, Preston's best friend. And I doubt he'd ever forgive me.

He's probably already joined the Gateway.

I slam down the magazine on the table in front of me and stare off into the dull lights on the roof. Preston probably hates me now. He probably thinks I am a fraud. He probably thinks that I am nothing more than a heartless, cold person. A liar.

But I had no choice...

I am woken from my realization when Mason, the lobby's intern secretary, approaches me.

"Elizabeth?" he says in his croaky, weak voice.

"Hmm?" I say to him in the most irritated tone I could muster. I don't understand how he got himself involved with the Lobby when he is the weakest and most nervous kid I know.

"The-the Devil would like to see you. Now. At this very moment. In his office," as he points down the hall, and scurries back to his desk.

I get up and walk down towards his room. *This is definitely something about Coley. Maybe congratulations for me? No, Mason wouldn't act that way if it were good news. Well maybe he would, because he's just a little wimp.*

I turn down the corridor, and walk towards the golden rimmed door that was his office.

"Come in."

I walk in to see a large desk with a pointy nosed lady sitting at it.

"Go directly in Elizabeth. Don't talk until he talks to you."

I walk towards the even fancier doorframe, and open it with a lot of care. I then walk lightly towards the red chair and sit down.

The Devil turns in his swivel chair and stares at me through his black sunglasses.

"Elizabeth," he says in his deep, emotionless voice. "I have heard of your murder this morning. And while that was not the situation I imagined for that dumb boy's death, I certainly can approve of it," he pauses for a moment, and although I cannot see his eyes, I can feel them staring into me. "I must say one thing now. You had Preston, who was just watching, all helpless, just over yonder. And you didn't bother to kill him as well, did you? NO SIREE, you did NOT. You just ran off here for cover. I have to say, a very weak reaction. Very weak. You agree that that was a poor reaction?" he says in a rhetorical question.

"Yes sir, I do fancy that it was not well planne," I say.

"Yes I do agree it was indeed NOT well executed there, but I have a way you may redeem yourself. My dear Elizabeth, I believe in you. I believe in the evil you possess. And I have a mission for you. One that shall redeem you! You, my dear Elizabeth, shall now kill Preston. Once. And. For all," he says, getting out of his chair still looking at me, and then slams the door behind him.

CHAPTER 22

The next morning when I woke up my mind was still messed up. I hoped that the past few days had been just a dream, a nightmare more like, but that idea was lost the very second I saw my surroundings. I was in a very plain room, white walls, a single-size bed with grey blankets, it was like many of the other Gateway rooms. But the Gateway did have many beautiful rooms also. I rose from the bed and stretched my arms. Following those actions I walked to the other side of the room. Near the door was a small cornertable, on it was a pair of clean clothes and a note:

"Get dressed and meet us in room 309. We have a lot to discuss and go over."

I looked over at the clothes they gave me and I felt as if I hadd seen them before. I looked back at the note and I understood why. They were Coley's.

"I know you probably think we're monsters for making you wear your dead friends clothes, but they were all we had in your size."

I sighed and put the note back. I took my time as I put on the pair of blue jeans, black shirt and plaid overshirt. It felt weird not just because they were Coley's, but I was used to wearing my school uniform. I left the overshirt unbuttoned, like Coley did when he wore them. It made me feel like he was still here. Just a little bit. When I was done getting ready, I walked out of the room with the note in my hand. Room 309. I was in 105 so I have a bit of a walk to do. I passed by hallways and hallways and just ended up at the entrance. What? I gave up on trying to find it myself, and went up to the front desk.

"Hey where could i find room 309?" I asked the lady sitting there.

She looked at my with a smile. It kinda freaked me out a little. It was too...nice. After a couple more seconds she looked down at her computer again. She started typing something and when pressed on her mouse. A whirring sound came from beside her. She pushed her rolling chair in that direction and to a black machine. A couple papers came out of it. She grabbed them and stapled them together after writing something down on them in red ink. She came back to me and handed me them.

"I've written the main rooms of the building and 309. You should be able to find where your headed," she told me.

"Thanks," I said as I started flipping through the pages. There were five of them. I found the way I needed to go and followed the red arrows the lady had drew. In about five minutes i made it to my destination. I knocked on he door and it was opened quickly by Maryanne. I smiled, but the feeling must not have been mutual.

"Finally, it only took you two hours," she said annoyance in her voice.

"Two hours?" I repeated surprised.

"Ya I left the note in your room at eight this morning," she said.

"You came in my room when I was sleeping?" I questioned her.

"It wasent my idea, trust me, Sawyer made me do it. I would have just let you walk around aimlessly in the Gateway trying to find us in your pyjamas."

"How am I not surprised?" I asked sitting down in one of the chairs that were placed around a large brown circular table. This was one of the rooms that was beautifully ornate with engraved wood designs and carvings on the button of the table and its feet. The room was light blue with a large window that had gold curtains tied back. It went well with the white ceiling and creme carpet. I sat between Maryanne and Sawyer, but we weren't the only ones there.

Sitting two chairs beside Sawyer was Dr. Chalice.

"What are you doing here?" I asked her. Her grey eyes looked me over.

"I have the best plan of action against the Devil," she said, robotic as always.

"Ya and she has been waiting for you to be here to tell us," Maryanne said. "It was the longest two hours of my life. The worse two hours of my life," she said exaggerating every word.

"You used to work for the Devil and kill for him, and this is the worst two hours of your life?" I said to her, my eyebrows raised. She looked me straight in the eyes.

"Yes. At least I was doing something, I have been sitting here for two hours, in silence because madame robot," she turned her head towards Dr. Chalice, "is bothered by the sound of breathing. And I couldent leave because you could have came in at anytime."

"I'm sorry?" I said.

"It's fine Preston," Sawyer said to me, "you needed the rest, a lot has happened in the past few days. And here, eat up."

He grabbed a plate of eggs and bacon from a small cart near him. I started eating as Dr. Chalice started speaking.

"So it's obvious, a war, a real fighting one has been set off. The Lobby versus The Gateway. The battle of the century that's certain. Here are the important things we need if The Gateways wants to win. A location for the battle that we have an advantage on. A good attack strategy with good fighters and weapons," she said in a powerful voice. Her eyes looked sharp and ready and her expression was the same.

"Well where do you suggest we fight?" asked Sawyer, "we don't exactly have very many options."

Dr. Chalice took a deep breath before saying her suggestion, "I suggest Coventry Garden," she said.

The room went silent. Coventry Garden? That was her idea. The school made by the Devil, where hundreds of innocent kids stayed.

"No!" I said, "It's basically controlled by the Devil. We would be giving him an advantage not us. Plus there are kids there. No."

"We would have the element of surprise. The Devil will never expect it. Plus, I think you forget Preston, I'm still the headmistress of the school. I could declare the school closed for some reason, the kids would be gone in a couple days then we have the school. I might not be the Devil but I know the school better than I know my own home," she said.

I leaned back into my chair, my opinion wouldn't change anything. Sawyer seemed to agree with her. They spoke some about the plan of attack.

"We send in a group here, here, and here," she spoke while pointing at a map of Coventry Garden, but our main focus is the Devil himself and His prime soldiers, His bodyguards. If we came get to the Devil, we can unseat him and hopefully, get a better one than this," she explained.

Better one than this?

"What do you mean?" I asked, "That makes no sense, you can't kill the Devil, you can't replace him," I said. Dr .Chalice looked over at Sawyer then at Maryanne.

"You haven't told him?" she asked. She was getting aggravated.

They both shook their heads.

"No!?, he's the Devil's son and you haven't told him that the Devil isn't an exact person," she yelled at Sawyer, who then rose from his chair.

"We don't know that he is his son," Sawyer said angrily.

"Yes he is. We know that because the Devil, Nar Echo, whatever you want to call him managed to get his mother, your then fiance to fall in love with him. And you're telling me, that wasn't enough for you to tell him the truth, that his father can be defeated and replaced?" they argued.

Maryanne was laughing at the situation and I was trying to wrap my head around it. The Devil isn't an exact person, it was a job of some sort.

"How can you replace the Devil with another one?" I asked, interrupting their argument.

They both turned to look at me.

CHAPTER 23

"There is a legend, one about how the Devil can be overthrown. It existed for centuries and came alive after the original Devil was defeated. At the time, one of the most known philosophers wrote a book on the Devil, his responsibilities and all that.

One night, when I was young and training at The Lobby, I got bored and decided that breaking into the forbidden section of the library would be fun. When I got inside I was in awe. There were so many dusty, old books that seemed to date from centuries before. I grabbed the biggest one. It had a fading red cover and thin pages, dissolving on the edges. It happened to be the book the philosopher wrote. I spent all night reading it, wondering why the Devil would keep the book informing everyone who read it on how to defeat him," Maryanne paused to take a breath before continuing.

"If you want to defeat the Devil, you need his most prized possession and the person you want to replace him. The person who will be his replacement must draw their blood on the possession, making a binding oath. The pain that comes with this event is cruel, the worst pain you could ever feel, like your heart and soul is being ripped from your body. It's what makes the Devil so heartless. If you manage to survive good for you, you're the new most hated person in the world. If you fail, then the devil you wanted to be replaced stays. It's pretty simple if you think about it," she said. She finished her story and grabbed a glass of water.

We all looked at eachother. I knew we were all thinking the same thing... What was the Devil's most prized possession? For a while we sat in silence, thinking over and over about what it could be. I looked down, my eyes landing on my ring. Elizabeth had one two. They were the Devil's before, they bind us together in a way.

"Mine and Elizabeth's rings. The Devil gave them to us when we were younger. They were his before. They are very important," I said to the group.

"I agree," Dr. Chalice spoke up. I was honestly surprised, "you're right Preston, I know a lot about the Devil, and those rings were the most important thing to him. They have to be what we need."

"There's only one problem," Maryanne said.

"What?" we asked her.

"You said Elizabeth has the other. And I don't know if you've been paying attention, but she's in The Lobby, against us. How are we going to get to her, let alone get the ring?" she asked. She brought up a good point.

"Does Elizabeth know you're with The Gateway?"

"No, of course not," she replied.

"Then you're probably our best chance at getting her ring," I told her.

She shrugged her shoulders. Dr. Chalice spoke up once again. And she spoke out to everyone in general as she said,

"Draw out Elizabeth, get her ring, destroy her's as well as yours...and the Devil will die."

CHAPTER 24

Our plan was made, Maryanne, Sawyer, Dr. Chalice and I would sneak into Coventry Garden tonight. We separated to get ready for any possible situation. Dr. Chalice was evacuating the school, so there would not be anyone there if the Devil showed his face. Sawyer was busy getting more people to come with us to the school. And Maryanne, well Maryanne was probably acting like herself. Meaning, that I didn't really know where she was or what she was doing. I was back in my room wondering what would happen tonight? I'd be back at school, but it wouldn't really be school. It would be more of a battlefield sort of thing. So no teachers yelling after me to get to class or giving me ten pages of homework due before twelve in the afternoon. We would be leaving in a couple of hours so I lay down on my bed. I closed my eyes, Maryanne would wake me up when we had to go, I'm gonna take a nap.

We weren't far from Coventry Garden now. And our group was walking quietly through the woods to get there.

Sawyer had managed to get five more people to come with us, meaning that nine of us were there. We traveled through the maze of trees and roots that threatened to trip us the second we took our eyes off the path. The darkness wasn't helping either, but we managed. After another ten minutes, we finally reached the school. I, alongside the others, walked past the iron gate that decorated the main entrance and up the stone path to the large wooden door.

Dr. Chalice looked for her key and unlocked the door. The school was as silent as a graveyard. And there was a slight eerie feeling lingering in the air. As if we weren't alone. Like at night, when all your lights are out and you can't help but wonder if there's something lingering in the shadows. I shook the idea out of my head, Dr. Chalice was the only one who had a key. Unless the Devil... no. I couldn't think that way.

I focused back on where we were being led. As we walked through the abandoned hallways, we saw the doors to classrooms and stairs every so often. It was shaping up to be a horror movie scene. Next thing you know some masked killer with a would jump out and try to stab me. My heart started beating faster at the very thought of that happening to me. I hit myself in the head, no I can't be a chicken, I cannot be a chicken.

"Boo!"

I screamed, jumping back. My heart was definitely beating a lot faster now. I put my hand on it as though it would actually do anything to help. Right beside me Mary-anne was laughing as quietly as she could, which was definitely not at all quiet.

"God, you look like you saw a ghost or something," she said with a grin plastered on her face.

"Well I nearly became one," I replied, my breath shaking just a little.

"Stop freaking out, it's just a school. Nothing bad is gonna happen, to you at leas," she told me. We kept on walking.

"To me? What does that mean?"

"It means that the chances that the Devil kills *you* is a lot less than, I dont know, Steve," she said gesturing to the blonde man Sawyer had managed to recruit.

"Thanks, I love being told I have a better chance at survival than Steve," I said somewhat sarcastically. And I would love to completely believe what she said were it true, but would the Devil really spare me if he had no need to? It dosent really matter if I'm his son or not? He's still the Devil.

We rounded a corner and into the auditorium, Dr. Chalice flicked a switch and lights above the seats turned on. But as the lights turned on, we saw that we were not the only ones there, waiting for a fight to arrive. We saw a group of people, they were maybe a couple more people than we were, they wore dark clothes but their skin was pale. Some did have darker tones but most looked quite alike. But their hair seemed to block all of their faces, so I wasn't able to recognize any of the boys or girls sitting. The last light that lit up was the central stage light. And when it did, I could instantly recognize the man standing there. His back was turned from us, but he turned when the lights appeared. Well dressed as always he spoke.

"I wondered when you would join us," he said, in a smooth voice.

"How did you get in here?" Dr. Chalice cried out in a raspy voice.

He chuckled.

"I own the school, you may be the headmistress, but I have a more important role in this school's creation,"he said.

They continued on this way. I looked at the others who joined him, and I could see their faces now. I scanned through them all, looking for someone without realizing it. And I took in a breath when I saw them, no, her. Her brown hair with red tint was let down. It was longer than before and a bit messy as if there was a crappy attempt to layer in it.

She must have realized I was staring because now her eyes were aligned with mine. That's all it took for me to realize I had to talk to her. I looked around the room, there were more people fighting. They had gotten up from their seats and were standing alongside the Devil. It must be confusing trying to understand what the others were saying. But it was the best distraction, nobody would notice if I left.

I looked back at Elizabeth, who hadn't taken her eyes off of me. I tilted my head to the side, to the direction of the exit. She nodded her head and got up quietly. I followed walking away from the group as fast and quietly as I could until I was one pace behind Elizabeth. I passed her and grabbed her wrist, pulling her behind me as we made our way out of the room.

CHAPTER 25

In the center of the chaos, a man in a white suit stood, face to face with one of his greatest foes. Both had known that this was coming; tonight, the tide would turn. One of them would not walk away from this with their life.

The headmaster's brow was sheathed in an icy rime of sweat. There was a fury in her eyes, and her mouth was set in a strict line.

They circled each other, predators defending their territories, her cold gray eyes never leaving his fiery, burning blue ones.

The Devil smiled his red vampire leer as he took a step towards Dr. Chalice.

"This is your last chance, Alma. Leave Coventry to me, return the boy, and you and your company will keep your miserable lives for the present."

In response, she reached into the pocket of her long coat and withdrew it holding a steel blade, its freezing surface seeming to hiss when it met the warmer air.

In an instant, a shining silver knife was in the Devil's hand as he lunged for Chalice. Her dagger leaped up to meet it, and sparks flew as the *clink* echoed throughout the cavernous room. The Devil let loose a gibbering, otherworldly roar, stabbing and slashing at his opponent as they danced and wove across the wooden floor. The other combatants gave them a wide berth, the aura of strangling nothing surrounding the Devil repelling any who might have interfered.

Something caught his eye amid the pandemonium, drawing his concentration away from Chalice with a snarl: His son had left the room, Elizabeth in tow. In that precious instant, the headmaster thrust her knife at his chest in one swift stroke, barely missing the man's vital organs and sinking into his shoulder as he made a vain attempt to dodge the blow. Gold stained the place where it hit, streaming along his side. The Devil howled in pain as she twisted it within the muscle, sweeping his legs out from under him as she did so. With a sickening thud, he sank to the floor, his knife skidding away across the wood. He raised his head calmly as Chalice's knife-tip pressed against the pale skin of his neck, producing a droplet of ichor that ran down, disappearing into his shirt collar. There was fury in the headmaster's eyes.

"This is my school, star-spawn, and I intend to keep it. Here's a counteroffer: depart from these grounds with the rest of your Lobby, return Elizabeth to us, and perhaps I will allow you to leave relatively unscathed. Do we have a deal?"

The Devil raised his hands in surrender, his lips hardly moving as he murmured assent to prevent further damage to his throat.

"Now GET OUT."

He smiled again, wistfully, "How I'll miss you, my dear Alma."

Metallic blood dribbled out from his mouth as its edges stretched, wider and wider in a horrible gape as his long red tongue, uncoiling, struck like a serpent, slamming into Chalice, wrapping around her neck and holding her aloft. Her eyes widened in shock as her mouth moved noiselessly, crimson forced out instead, landing with a splash in the spreading gold pool. The headmaster's legs and arms flailed in an effort to escape from the doom before her. Her knife fell to the floor, piercing the boards.

Any semblance of humanity had drained from the Devil as his face split open vertically like skin peeling back from a scab, teeth elongating into row after row of sharklike fangs, receding deep into his throat as thick spittle formed a column to the roof of his mouth. At the back of this tunnel burned the searing light of a thousand dying stars.

YOU ARE MINE THEY ALL ARE MINE THEY'RE ALL DOWN HERE WITH ME ALMA ARTHUR CANDEN AND JOHN DERUSA AND SWEET LITTLE BETTY DOBBINS ALL DEEP IN MY LOBBY WHERE THE STARS CAN'T REACH COME WITH US WE'VE BEEN WAITING...

Chalice ceased struggling, her legs dangling inert below her, as she stared blankly at the hypnotic, alien fire. Her swollen tongue, like a massive slug, jutted from between her blue lips.

HOW YOU'VE MISSED THEM ALL THOSE YOU'VE LOST THEY'RE ALL HERE ALL HERE WAITING OH HOW THEY CAN'T WAIT COME WITH ME DOWN IN THE DARK COME WITH USSSS...

Though his terrible mouth never moved, the Devil's voice echoed through her mind, melding with those of her fallen friends, high and screeching and monstrously inhuman, garbling out a single word: ***FAREWELL.***

The last thing Chalice saw as her neck snapped like a brittle, hollow bone was the light filling her vision was Arthur Canden, a dreadful leer plastered on his lipless face, the edges of which had been nibbled away by adventurous fish, beckoning to her with one waxy, smooth mannequin's hand worn away by decades at the bottom of a pond.

The Devil released her as she went limp, her glasses cracking in a fine web as they hit the floor.

Regarding his fallen foe reflectively for a moment, he bent down over her broken body. Sliding the signet ring, emblazoned with the Coventry crest, smoothly off her left hand, he placed it in the breast pocket of his ruined suit. Turning on his heel, the Devil strode towards the door, beyond which, away from the fighting, Preston begged the love of his life for what he was certain was the one thing in the world that could end the Devil's reign, once and for all.

CHAPTER 26

In my life, never in all my moments on earth did I think that I could have heard a silence so strong. A silence just sitting, watching as its long sharp claws latch themselves to my mind. A silence only broken from Elizabeth standing and walking across to the disheveled pipes sitting in the corner of this small storage closet. The pipes may have formerly been used to give the students of Coventry cool air during hot summer days or perhaps carry water through to the water fountains. But now, even these pipes were a weapon. Another intriguing tool for a new atrocity to be performed. The thought that this may be just the reason Elizabeth is walking to the pipes puts me on edge. Lifting me from my trance. The waves crash on me all at once. The everlasting screams and yells pouncing through the eight inches of wood securing my safety for the moment. The sirens of the school are flaring and flashing desperate to keep us all in order. I stand. My legs tired and stiff but no thought of taking a break from thought or worry crosses my mind. As much as I wish I could trust Elizabeth I know I can't. I cautiously work my way over to the pipes where Elizabeth is standing unmoving.

"Elizabeth?" No response. I walk to her side and speak again. "Elizabeth, I, I know this may not seem logical for you but if you are even somewhat interested in helping defeat the Devil... you need to give me your ring."

She sporadically turns towards me, her eyes aflame and suffocating. "Are you crazy?? Give you the rings so you can what? Kill me? Kill the Devil? Has it ever crossed your mind that maybe I don't want the Devil dead? Maybe that I need the years that have led to today to matter? Maybe I want my side to win this war?" she smiled softly, "If you kill the Devil, kill those rings, you might just kill me Preston," she says.

I stand gaping at her. How could everything we had been through lead to her refusing, to her refusing the opportunity to defeat the Devil?

"You cannot seriously be saying that you are more worried of the slightest chance that you might be killed by this rather than the countless amount of lives it could save?"

"Am I not allowed to worry about my own life? I have murdered, Preston! I have seen life in a human drain slowly until their eyes are left gray. I don't want that to happen to me. I don't want my eyes to turn blank, not yet."

"Elizabeth, I would never do this if I was not sure that there was a way we could survive in the end. I know that no matter what happens when the rings are destroyed, we will find each other, dead or alive."

She chuckles softly as she removes the golden ring glinting from the silver light of the pipes.

"I am now putting my life on your finger Preston, what you choose to do with it is no longer in my control."

She walks silently from the room and back out into the roaring flame of battle. As the door opens there is a distinct cry. A cry clearly from Maryanne. A cry not of anguish but anger. A cry of fury. Running back out from the room I see that the battle has ceased for the moment. No clear victor but one clear sight. The tall slender body of Dr. Chalice lies in the center of the auditorium, a bright stage light shining over her lifeless body.

CHAPTER 27

I sit on the stiff couch, my hand shielding my eyes from the rooftop light, the back of my head presses onto the cold wall. We sit there in silence. The darkness is a calming sight for me, while nothing else is. Sawyer is pacing around the room, counting on his fingers, and mumbling in a form of gibberish. Maryanne sits on the couch across from me, her eyes staring emptily at Sawyer.

I rotate myself on the couch and look at Sawyers' nervous pacing. The guy never seems at rest, always in a nervous state. When you're defeated, it's easier to just be defeated.

"That fight was so dumb. If Chalice hadn't died, I would've killed her for starting it so suddenly," Maryanne mumbles. Sawyer pauses from his pacing to give her a look.

I re-adjust myself on the couch, and suddenly, I feel a sharp ping in my throat. I felt my pocket and pulled out Elizabeth's ring. I had forgotten I had had this, I was so tired.

"What'cha got there Preston?" Maryanne says, sitting up. Sawyer looks over from his pacing.

"Is that the *other* ring?" Sawyer asks in slight shock.

"Uh, yes."

Sawyer lifts out his hand towards the ring, but I pull it back into my chest.

"But listen. If we break this, you see, if it breaks at all, it will kill Elizabeth. And, and, I'm just not ready to do that. There must be another way to kill him. What is a little more time to lose anyway?"

Maryanne nods at that, as she didn't want to lose Elizabeth either. Sawyer opens his mouth to say something, but then rethinks his words.

"I guess," he finally says, and he goes back to pacing. I roll back on the couch, the ring clutched in my hand.

But just then, the door clangs open. "I don't care if that ring will kill me."

I know the voice immediately, and I shoot up to see Elizabeth in the doorway.

"I don't care what will happen, but we need to destroy the Devil once and for all. We must finish what we have begun."

"We?"

"Yeah we. I'm with you now."

I try to hide my excitement, but I then notice Sawyer staring at Elizabeth in an untrustworthy manner.

"How do we know that the Devil did not send you to try and get information from us?" he says, in a very Sawyer-like way.

"Elizabeth isn't on the most trusted terms with the Devil right now so I doubt he would send her of all people to go get information from us. And surely she wouldn't betray her best friend," she says staring at Elizabeth in a threatening fashion.

"Well I don't know if the devil would send me or not, but I assure you that I want him out. But I do need to go now, I didn't check out and if I am gone for too long He may suspect something. But, to prove I am trustworthy, I'll try with all my power to be back in the next 3 days. And if not, destroy those rings. Now I really gotta run," she says as she scurries back into a dark hallway.

Sawyer stands there quizzically, then a realization occurs, "Who let her in to begin with?"

CHAPTER 28

As I tangle my way through the pitch black woods, I come upon the rusty pothole by mere accident, as I banged my foot on it. Instead of continuing to be blind through the woods, I lift up the emergency entrance and go down the creaking ladder.

When I get to the bottom of the ladder, I open up the door to immediately see Mason running towards me.

"Where have you been? The Devil has been on a rampage, called an emergency meeting *because* of you! And where were you off at 4 in the morning?"

Mason was dragging me towards the office in a nervous pants. "The Devil was about to kill me if I didn't find out where you were before 7! Where in god's name were you?" He was now looking up at me through his thick glasses, truly scared.

"I was taking care of some business," I said and walked ahead of him and went through the golden entrance to the devils office. When I walked inside, I was shocked to see John DeRusa sitting in the first chair in front of the devil.

"There you are Elizabeth. Have a seat. You're late," He said. I was surprised that he didn't ask where I was, but at the same time, relieved, as I had not fully made my excuse yet.

"Ok, so where were we?" The Devil asks in a monotone voic,. "ah, yes, John here has requested to speak with me about our good friend Preston."

I look at John, still surprised to see him here.

"He, with the help of our new spy, Steve, believes that Preston is a larger threat than we expected," as He motions to a man I had never seen before to speak. I assumed he was Steve.

"Yes, as the new spy, I learned Preston has stolen your ring Elizabeth. How did that come to happen, may I ask?" he looks straight at me. I flick at my finger, acting surprised that that had occurred.

"I-I have not realized it was missing?," I say in staged surprise.

"Well it is indeed missing. And that is a large issue, as you see, those rings offer a safety concern to our Devil here. I learned that Preston stole it from you during the battle. Don't trust him," John says.

John, in his ghostly form, speaks up, "Elizabeth, I've spoken with the Devil, and he has said that you must move up the day of the murder. Or else, if those rings are broken, the Devil's life will be in danger."

CHAPTER 29

Preston sat, lost in thought, under the dim light of a shaded lamp as his pen scratched against paper:

December 21

Elizabeth has been gone three days. No news from her. Is she alright? What has she found? Does he know? If she doesn't come back soon, I 'll go find her. Whatever he's done to her

A knock came at the door. At his response, Marry-anne entered. She looked worn and faded, a shadow of her former self. Without preamble, she said gravely:

"He's here."

Preston rose to his feet, uncomprehending.

"Your father's waiting for you, Preston. Down by the pond. He asks that you come alone."

"How did he get here? Is - is Elizabeth with him?"

Maryanne shook her head, "Just him."

"What does he want?"

"He says he just wants to talk."

"Why should we trust him? After all he's done, after what he did to Chalice?"

"We need to know what he is planning. This is now our best chance of getting any kind of intelligence, until Elizabeth returns," she says.

Preston sighed, "I'll meet him."

"We'll have soldiers stationed at the windows and in the trees nearby, in case he tries anything. If he does," she gripped the hilt of the knife at her side, "we'll be ready."

"Very well. Let's go see the Devil."

* * *

Behind the school, at the center of a dense clearing, the Devil paced, the dark pond glistening beside him under a blanket of ice. The sun was setting behind him, bathing his angular features in a bloody halo. Unperturbed by the freezing temperature, he wore nothing but a slim black suit. As the doors at the far end of the courtyard creaked open, he grew still, patiently awaiting his host's arrival.

A boy was walking across the dead and frosted leaves, each step's ensuing *crack* echoing through the cold evening air. A strong gust of icy wind screamed through the air. Drawing his coat more tightly around him, Preston strode on, reaching the side of the pond opposite the Devil.

Almost shouting to be heard over the wind, the boy said:

"You said you wanted to talk."

When the Devil spoke, just above a whisper, it was as though he was speaking directly into Preston's ear. His lips barely moved as he did so.

"Before I met your mother, I was broken. The Lobby had become divided, under attack from within and without, its angles disrupted. I grew weak," he gave a shudder, "and for a time I thought that it was all over. One night, while I wandered in search of any who would take me in, I had a vision, and I knew that this girl would be my salvation. I scoured the land for her, this girl I hardly knew. It consumed me. My enemies took advantage of my temporary weakness by trying to end me. I escaped, badly wounded, and awoke on your mother's doorstep with a terrible case of amnesia" He continued.

"For millions of years I've been alone, moving from body to body to body, my only companions, my Lobby. I chose to live this way; I shudder to think of what would happen should I be reunited with my old folk. I was isolated, reviled, shunned, treated as anathema by the ungrateful creatures who owe their very existence to me. Until I met her," He said.

"She took me in, nurtured me, protected me. She was my friend, my only true friend is this universe. I felt so... so loved. And then that man, Jonathan, tried to ruin it all. And for a short time, I thought he had been successful" He said almost lovingly.

"I went on a walk with him, tried to discover his intentions. When he laughed at me, something snapped. I don't remember the rest of that night, only that he ended up dead in a roadside ditch," continuued the Devil.

"After the investigation died down, I returned to your mother, and we lived together in perfect happiness until you were born," He said.

"You were the perfect child, and she loved you more than anything in the world. Even me. I grew resentful, and began to fear that I had not been your father, after all. Despite that, we may have managed to coexist peacefully were it not for my most loyal servant," continued the Devil.

"She tracked me down, found me at our house, told me who I was, that all who remained thought me dead. It all came back after that. The untold millennial..."

"As you grew, I spent more and more time away from home, away from her. I could not leave her permanently; I still hoped what I had hoped all along, that she would save me in the end," He went on.

"When she told me that she knew who I was, I was furious. I lashed out, and killed her." A single small tear rolled down a cheek bereft of any wetness from the icy chill. "I killed her, and I lost you, and for that I will suffer for eternity, until the last star grows cold and fades forever into the void, never to return. Oh, how I've missed you, my son," flinging the tear from his face with the back of his hand, he regained his composure.

Preston spoke at last, his voice harsh.

"What do you want?" The Devil was near him now, his breath hardly noticeable when it made contact with the frigid air.

"My dear boy, I have an offer to make you. Do you remember those rings I gave you and Elizabeth all those years ago?"

In response, Preston held out his hand, opening his palm to reveal the silver bands, their shapes imprinted into his skin in thin red circles. The Devil smiled.

"As you know, they were your mother and my wedding rings. They contain a bit of each of us, and as we are both aware, they are quite capable of returning me to true mortality. I want you to give them to me," the Devil said.

"And why should I do that? Why should I not destroy them here, as you watch?"

"Elizabeth tells me that you promised to wait until she returns. As it stands, you might just keep waiting."

"What have you done with her?"

"Don't you worry, she's quite well. In fact, she wishes you would join us. We have much to discuss."

"Of course, you do realize that I am not the only life at stake? Break those rings, and you will find out just how fragile your dear friends in my Lobby are. Give them to me, and I will ensure their safety."

"I- they know the risk," I say.

"So cold, Preston. Would you really make that choice for them? Condemn them all to an early grave? Is that really what Chalice would want? What Elizabeth would? Come now. Surely you're more reasonable than that. I would hate to see another needless conflict end in such an unfortunate fashion. I don't want war, Preston."

The Devil extended his hand.

For an instant, Prestons hand paused midway to the Devil's, the rings gripped tightly between its index finger and thumb.

"I'm sorry, Elizabeth," I say.

Recognition appeared on the Devil's face as he lunged for the boy, meeting his ready fist and going down, sliding and falling on the ice. Rising laboriously to his feet, he charged again at Preston, countless emaciated arms unfurling from within his suit.

Preston released the rings, and brought his boot down upon the brittle metal with a sound like a thousand mirrors shattering.

As black viscous blood bubbled out from the rings' crushed remains, the Devil fell to his knees, clutching his head as his inhuman scream echoed throughout the courtyard. Around him, the air seemed to waver and shine, an aurora of flickering light, its shape almost humanlike...

A deafening crack pierced the Devil's screams.

Preston and the Devil froze, and simultaneously looked down to see the crimson flower blooming across the Devil's chest.

With the end of one long finger, he gently touched the spreading stain, looking at his fingertip with a childish amazement, slowly turning to rage.

He stood shakily once more, his hands clenching and unclenching, jaw working furiously. He snarled. His eyes began to shine.

Blinding light exploded outwards from his chest, and Preston collapsed, stunned, his sight full of flames. When his eyesight recovered, the Devil was gone.

CHAPTER 30

Murmuring had broken all around the Lobby. I knew what that meant, the Devil was back. Someone had seen him walk to his office and spread the word. Apparently, he didn't look too good. I got up and made my way to see him. I was hoping, deeply praying, that he was on his deathbed, that Preston had done something. Not with the rings though, that option was only eligible the second midnight struck. And I trust Preston, I know he would keep his word. He loved me, he wouldn't risk my life. But... no i had to trust him, I do trust him.

I knocked on the door to his office and a voice, unrecognizable, told me to enter. I gasped.

In his tall chair the Devil sat. But you could barely recognize him. His skin was an icky white-gray color with dark purple under his eyes. His formerly proper cut dark hair was not tangled and decorated in silver streaks. His gray suit was unbuttoned and a couple seams were ripped, he was a mess. There was a mysterious blood stain on it also. The blood was a mix of gold and red, which I had never seen before. Red blood. Slowly becoming the more potent color.

"If you're done staring I could use some help," He said in a snappy voice.

His voice was breathless and had no more real control in it. But I tore my gaze from him and rushed to a cabinet on the other side of the room. I opened it and grabbed the first aid kit. I then helped him take off the blazer.

"Where did the blood come from?" I asked, I had to pretend I cared.

He grunted.

"I don't know," is all he responded.

I just took his blazer from him and threw it into the bathtub that came with the bathroom connected to his office. I ran hot water and added some soap and a little bleach to the mixture, before I went back to the man who looked on the verge of dying.

"I'm going to clean your smaller cuts now, this might hurt," I said.

I put a bit of rubbing alcohol on a piece of cloth and gently patted it on his cuts. He took in a sharp breath, pride stopping him from doing any more than that. I kept doing so and soon he just stared off into the distance.

"Is everything okay?" I asked. What was I thinking? He obviously wasn't.

"Preston destroyed the rings, aware it could kill you," He said, a small smile desperately trying to break across his face.

No. No, no, no, he couldn't have. No, we had a deal. He did not. The Devil is lying to me, trying to get me mad at Preston, I trust Preston. But the Devil has never lied to me so why would he start now?

"No he didn't, he loves me, he would never risk my life," I argued. It was a terrible choice doing so. Arguing with the Devil I mean.

"Foolish girl, you really think he cares if you die? If it means he wins and I lose? He will do anything. Even risk your life by destroying both rings. Look what happened to me, it didn't even work! He risked your life, for nothing. You mean nothing to him. Why can't you see that?!"

His voice was getting louder once more, as if the injured man was leaving.

"Because Preston loves me more than anything, he's proved that a million times and all I've ever done is taken it for granted, used it against him. It took a while but I now understand how he feels,"I said.

My voice was doing the opposite as his, it was getting softer and softer. The Devil laughed softly.

"You love him," He said simply, shaking his head.

His laugh got louder and louder, until I closed my eyes.

"Stupid girl, you cannot love. Look at DeRusa, you came close and then you killed him. Your father, dead. Your mother, dead. Your old orphanage, mine. And you think the same won't happen to Preston? He is cursed, but can't you see? What you are is the worst. You're stuck in a never ending loop, where everyone and everything you care about gets lost, dies, belongs to me. I own you Elizabeth Grey, and you can't escape, no matter how hard you try. No matter how much you kill. I'm the Devil. And you're just a girl, stuck working for me. No matter how much you try to escape, you come back don't you?"

"No I don't," I say. My breath was shaking and silent tears left red under my eyes.

"Then tell me one time you didnt come back," He challenged me.

I pulled at my hair, killing my mind, desperately searching for a time where I didn't care about what the Devil thought of me. But I couldn't. I was loyal, to death. Literally, I could die in a minute, in a day and it would be because of Preston. Because I fell in love. Because I trusted him. I can't trust him. I want to, I yearn for it. But the Devil is right. I always end up in the same situation. I care about someone, I love them, and I lose them, kill them, they get away from me. It's taken me years for me to realize it, and it's the Devil that has cleared my mind.

Sobbing, I can hear myself cry. And the Devil just sits in front of me, smirking, content with the realization he has given me.

"Preston destroyed the rings, knowing that it could kill you, Elizabeth. What do you plan on doing?," He asked.

I looked up at him. He still looked beat up, like a corpse, but he was still the same. He never let anyone see him weak, he would never. And that applied even to me.

"So what are you going to do? You can help me survive, or you can go help your so-called love, who not only broke a promise, but gave you that nice gray spot in the palm of your hand," the Devil said angrily.

I quickly looked at my palms. And I broke even more, the same color as the Devil's was, on my palm. Just a little, but it was there. I could die.

"So what's it going to be, Miss. Grey?"

The uncomfortable familiarity that came with the name was terrible. Could I trust that Preston had an amazing reason for doing this to me? Or would I stay with the Devil, as I always have?

CHAPTER 31

I sat still by the lake. A cool breeze pushing past the trees and into the clearing, making ruffles in the water. And for the first time in a while, I felt at peace. The rings were gone, they left only their smoldering remains by my feet and they had hurt the Devil. He had disappeared in a hurry, hopefully he was passing on, going to a different place. One where he would be dead, and everyone else happy.

I looked at the water. A small fish had jumped out and dived back in. And soon the sound of water splashing slightly wasn't the only sound I could hear. Someone was walking over to me, but I didn't take my eyes away from the fish swimming. I saw from the corner of my eye the familiar shortly cut hair. Maryanne. We sat in silence, watching the water as if there was nothing else to do. That was until she broke it.

"Is it done? Is *he* gone?" she asked me.

"I did it. But I'm not certain if he's dead or not. He disappeared right after I destroyed the rings," I replied to her.

Her shoulders fell.

"So we don't know if it worked. Great. It's the most important thing we need to know, so of course we don't. We don't know if we destroyed the Devil. We don't know if Elizabeth is okay," she says. Elizabeth

Of course. Was she alright? Did I hurt her? What if I did, does she hate me for using the rings? She trusted me and I can't know if she still does now. Especially if she is with the Devil. God, that would be terrible. What will he do to her? What will she do? Help him or me?

"Preston!" I snapped my head towards Maryanne.

"What?" I asked her. She rolled her eyes.

"I know you have a lot on your mind Preston, you have the right to after what happened. But you could have just killed your girlfriend and one of my best friends," she argued.

"She's not technically my girlfriend," I whispered.

"Well she certainly won't be if you killed her!"

"I didn't kill her!" I said.

"How do you know? You destroyed the rings, Elizabeth is connected to one. If you killed the Devil, what says that you didn't do the same to her?" She pointed to me.

"I've known Lizzie for a lot longer than you have. And she always does what she says she will. And she hasn't contacted us. Chances are she's dead," Maryanne said harshly.

"Or she betrayed us," I said.

"She wouldn't do that" she said.

"How do you really know? You hadn't seen her in a long time because she was at Coventry Garden and you were in the Gateway. I destroyed the rings without her knowing, we had a deal, a promise. And she trusts me with all she has, if I've broken that trust what will I do? Try to gain it back? It's Elizabeth! I love her, I really do. So much it kills me when I even think about losing her. Now what if I actually have Maryanne? What if I lost the only thing I've ever loved this much? The one person I would do absolutely anything for? If I have, what will I do with myself? I've already lost my best friend. And if I lost my love, what do I have left? What is keeping me here on earth?" I asked her.

"I don't know Preston. People are all different. But we, I, can't afford to give you hope that she's alive and well. Especially if she's dead, or near-dead. I would be lying. And that's not what you need right now," she replied.

"What do I do?" I asked her. She sighed.

"When my father died, I was a mess..." I looked at her, I had to tilt my head since she was a couple inches taller than me. "I refused to talk to anyone, my mother included. I cut my friends out of my life, hid in my room. I was nine. So at that age, kids were difficult. You forgot to talk to your friend for a couple days and you weren't considered friends anymore. So the week I went back to school, people just stared. They had the right to. I shut everyone out. It's okay, I survived. I mean, I am here, aren't I?"

"If you don't mind me asking, how did you get into the Lobby training program thing?" I asked.

"I don't mind. And well, my mom owed the Devil a favor. She was in debt. And I don't really care, we were not very close. But she wanted my father back. She was depressed, worse than me. So you can probably guess what she did," I nodded my head.

"She went to the Devil. Got him back, but at a price."

"Yup. Preston, I hate to say this, but the chance that Elizabeth is well is very slim. She's either dead, hurt or extremely lucky."

I looked away from the girl and back to the water. And as I looked at it, perfectly still, it rippled. Ever so slightly, if you weren't looking you would not have noticed. And then it did it again. The group of fish that swam freely in the center rushed to the sides. They hid where they could, under algae and behind rocks. They were soon invisible to the eye. A cold wind blew and I shivered. What was happening. And then, by magic. Elizabeth was there. Standing on the other side of the lake. Right where the bleeding Devil had.

CHAPTER 32

Preston stood still, staring across the lake at his love. For a moment, no one spoke.

Maryanne was the first to move, grabbing Preston's hand and walking around the frozen pond to meet the new arrival.

"Welcome back, Elizabeth," said Maryanne.

Maryanne moved to embrace her as Elizabeth walked past without sparing her a glance, ending in front of Preston. Raising her gloved hand, she slapped Preston across the face, his head turning with the force of the blow.

"How could you do it, after you promised not to? You said you wouldn't destroy the rings until I returned. HOW COULD YOU?"

Preston was silent, cupping the side of his face in his hand.

"I trusted you. And you broke your promise."

"I - I'm sorry, Elizabeth."

"You're SORRY? Oh, I'm so glad that you're SORRY for doing something that, for all you knew, would have killed me. Until now, you might have still thought that you had. We had a *promise.*"

"I know. The Devil... he wanted me to give them to him. I thought - I thought he had done something to you, found out, even killed you. It might have been our last chance to be rid of him forever. And I took it."

"It wasn't your choice to make!"

As Elizabeth prepared to strike Preston again, Maryanne interposed herself between the two of them. Elizabeth glared furiously at her.

"Please, try to understand, Elizabeth. We all knew the risk. I'm sorry, but if any one of us - the people of the Gateway - could do anything to put a chip in the Devil's defenses, maybe even bring him down, it would be worth it. We must be ready to give everything in service of our cause," Maryanne stated.

Maryanne gently took hold of Elizabeth's raised hand, lowering it without resistance. She sighed.

"Come with me. Both of you. I have to show you two something."

Elizabeth and Preston followed her silently away from the pond, towards the back door of Coventry Gardens. At the top of several flights of stairs, before the door to Dr. Chalice's office, Maryanne paused. She stared at the name on the door for a few seconds, mustering her strength, before entering.

Striding over to the polished desk at the back of the room, she opened the top drawer.

"Maryanne Griffin."

The floor behind the desk slid backwards, revealing the stone staircase below. Maryanne turned to face her companions.

"What are you waiting for?" she asked?

Tentatively, they followed, Preston trailing meekly behind Elizabeth.

* * *

"Welcome to the Gateway, Elizabeth. Preston, welcome back."

She had led them through the twisting, dark corridors under Coventry, in which dim electric lights sat at regular intervals along the walls and casted long shadows upon the floor, opening into the great hall in which they now stood. Rows of marble columns shot into the air, supporting some unseen ceiling far above. Stars twinkled out of the blackness in intricate constellations. Ghostly blue fire crackled in sconces. Murals of people long dead adorned the walls, spears and bows and knives and pistols in their hands, the style changing from figure to figure. At the far end of the hall, near a painting of a gray-haired bespectacled woman, was a dais, on which sat a massive altar, its pitted black stone polished to a shine. Carved into it was the image of a burning eye, encircled by two concentric rings. Noticing the direction of Preston's gaze, Maryanne informed him:

"It's a meteorite. It fell in this spot, thousands of years ago."

She spread her arms.

"For centuries, we have gathered here, in the shadows, planning, biding our time. This is the core of the Gateway.

This is where it was born, when a small group of people became aware of the Devil's influence and saw this rock as a sign. Of what, their successors can only guess. Over the years, the organization has grown. Un - Under Chalice, we began our program at Coventry, keeping our eyes out for any who we might recruit into our ranks.

"Since our founding, we've worked tirelessly to undermine the Devil and his schemes. We've rarely been in an all-out war; most of our operations are small, involving only a few agents, chipping away at his defenses. The time has come once more; the Devil has been weakened. We must strike swiftly, before he can recover from this latest blow.

"Here's what we know about our enemy: he's ancient. Older than any of us, older than humanity, possibly. He came from up there."

Maryanne pointed upwards at the glittering stars as they walked onwards, passing portrait after portrait. A hook-nosed man in regal garments glared imperiously at them from his frame.

"He has seen the rise and fall of empires, pulling the strings of time. If we don't stop him, he'll manipulate countless more. He is powerful; of that there is no doubt. Up until very recently, he was just about immortal. His Lobby protects him and carries out his will. What you have seen of him, what we can actually kill, is only the tip of the iceberg. The rest waits below the surface, poised for its ascension once more to godhood."

They had reached the end of the hall, and presently stood at the foot of the small flight of steps leading up to the dais.

"This is where the Devil must meet his end, upon the sky-born altar. One of you will bring him down, when the time comes."

She turned to face them with a grave countenance.

"But I fear whoever does so may end up replacing him."

CHAPTER 33

Steven Roy Leighman stood across from the weary shell of a man the Devil now was. The Devil's eyes wandered around the room, in a daze of disarray. His black suit was wrinkled and ripped on the wrists. Black circles had formed around his now dull gray eyes. His skin was wrinkled at the brow, as he muttered unintelligible words to himself. But suddenly, he stood up with great prowess, with a sense of power that he no longer possessed.

Steve looked away from the window which he had been day dreaming upon to look at the disheveled man.

"Sir, would you like a glass of water?" He started walking away from the room, in preparedness to go get some fine water for his master, but a small move of the wrist by the Devil, and Steve returned in front of him. The Devil gestured his hand down at Steve and smiled with a devilish grin at his obedience. He walked to a cabinet, took out a small elixir and limped his way back towards his golden rimmed desk.

The devil looked at the emptiness that now possessed Steven Roy Leighman, and grinned. The man who sat across from him was only there to serve at that moment. For he had made him so.

Steven Roy Leighman was the Sherlock Holmes of the states. From Annapolis, Maryland, he knew how to make everything go into place. No mystery could stump him. Not one. By the time he was 23, he was the head police chief of the entire state of Maryland, and by the age of 27, he ran the entire police force.

He was enlisted by the Gateway to figure out who had robbed them, in a relatively minor case. He solved it in 5 minutes, piecing together the staged situation. Because in reality, Sawyer DeRusa wanted this as a tryout for a new member. But Steven Roy Leighman was unwilling to join, for he was still rising in his home country. But that didn't stop the Gateway from pleading for him to help them with their largest mysteries concerning the Devil.

And the Lobby did want this modern day Sherlock Holmes as well, but instead of pleading like a child, the Devil came up with an ingenious plan. He bribed Steven Roy Leighman to come to the Lobby, coerced him into his office, a little chit chat, and then he offered Steven Roy Leighman a drink. Inside the drink, contained a potion that the Devil had brewed himself. This potion kept Steven Roy Leighman's wits and intelligence, but installed at the forefront of his brain, a desire to serve the Devil, and to never deny anything He would say. And just like that, the world's wittiest man was in the palm of the Devil's hand. And, knowing the Gateway's wants for Steven Roy Leighman, he sent Steve to the Gateway, and, with no questioning needed, he was allowed into one of the highest position imaginable.

And now the Devil laughed at his ingenious plan which had worked so amazingly, so extraordinarily well, that he felt he must add an encore to this. He got up, shook the black blue elixir and handed it to Steve. Steve took the elixir from the Devil's hand and sniffed it. He had a slight repulsion from the stench but he then swallowed the elixir. His eyes bulged at the taste, but he kept strong. After a minute of nausea, he felt normal. He looked at the Devil, who sat with his hands on his chin, staring back at Steve with a death stare.

"Why did I drink that?" Steve asked the Devil. Instead of answering, the devil just laughed with a creepy smile pasted across his face. Then all of a sudden, Steve eye started twitching. And all of a sudden he morphed into the man who stared back at him.

"What?" Steve looked down at himself, then at the grinning Devil in front of him, "I-I am you?" he asked.

"Indeed you are, Steven Roy Leighman. Indeed you are! Now you have the power to change yourself into anyone you wish to be. This is the first time I have used this elixir on an agent! And I'm glad to see it worked. Ah, that combination of Iodine and Apple juice never fails," He congratulated Himself.

He got up, feeling stronger than he had in a while, his grin still plastered on his face.

"Now, Steve, you now have the most important task anyone can have. You're going break the Gateway, from the inside!"

The devil holds up a photo of Maryanne, and implies with his hand for Steve to go on. Steve stands there for a moment, unsure of how to morph, but then all of a sudden, he sprouts into Maryanne.

"Go Steve. You know what to do," the Devil said and his grin grew. And grew. And grew. A slight chuckle.

CHAPTER 34

I sat alone in my room, thinking. There were many scenarios, possibilities, ways to what we were to do next. We could leave the Lobby alone altogether and just disappear, we could bring an army to their doorstep and start a physical war. I could go alone and sacrifice my life for the world. But there were loopholes in those ideas. Little things that could turn the whole thing around, making everything worse. I needed someone, not everyone. Just one, maybe two, people that would be willing to sacrifice themselves with me to save the world. But those people are pretty hard to find these days. I don't need anyone stabbing me in the back. Literally and figuratively.

As I was pondering these ideas, I heard a knock on my door. I looked up at it then told them to come inside. I watched Elizabeth open the door tentatively and peek her head in. She saw me and then proceeded to enter my room.

"You ok?" I asked her.

"Ya, I just wanted to make sure you weren't super busy before I actually came in," she replied, giving me a shy smile.

"Nope, just thinking," I told her.

"About what?"

"About what our next move is going to be. It's like a game of chess we're playing with the Devil. He took most of our pawns off of the board and one of our more valuable pieces. We've done pretty similar to them but whatever we do we just can't seem to capture the king," I explained to her as she sat on my bed.

"Well then, if we're playing this like a game of chess, we need a plan. We haven't had a real foolproof plan yet, unlike Him. That's how He's taking us off of the board so easily, we are not thinking of everything. About everyone on His side working for Him, protecting Him," she inquired.

She was right, we haven't thought about everyone else in the game. It wasn't just us and the Devil. It was us and our army against Him and his. And we needed a plan.

"Well then what do you suggest our next move is?" I asked her.

"Sometimes you need to just go for it the second you see an opportunity. Even if it means you might fail, it's worth trying," She told me, and I nodded my head.

"Then who's it going to be?" I asked her, "you and me?"

"We would be the best people for the job, and even if we just weaken him more it's a success, others could finish the job if we don't make it back," she said, I agreed with her.

"So what is the plan? We can't just walk into the Lobby. The Devil most definitely knows you're with us and against him now, so you can't be seen there unless you have a deathwish. And same for me, only they might not kill me in an instant. They probably know that I'm the Devil's son so..." I stated.

"The Gateway should have something, a weapon or some magic thing that could help us. And if not, we just sneak in. Kill anyone who sees us or is in our way," She said, she was standing up, pacing back and forth now. Looking at me intently, searching for a reaction.

"Kill them?" I repeated.

"Yes Preston. These are people who have done terrible things. These are people who work for the Devil. And some aren't even people, well, you remember the Lobby," she said.

I nodded my head once more.

"The point is, they will tell the Devil we are there if they see us, and if we don't do anything about it, it could ruin everything. It's the best option we have," she said.

I sighed, I hoped that we would meet nobody in our little venture.

"Okay, fine, I agree. But it's only if the Gateway doesn't have anything they can give us. And speaking of the Gateway they are having a council meeting tomorrow where we can tell them our plan. Talk about good timing," I said the last part with a small chuckle.

Now let's hope they agree to our proposal.

CHAPTER 35

A semicircular wooden conference table occupied the majority of the small meeting room. Thirteen seats, twelve plastic folding chairs and one larger wooden armchair like a throne in the center, were set about its periphery; all but two were occupied by a member of the Gateway's inner circle. A podium had been set before the table.

Sawyer sat stiffly in the central chair, looking exceedingly uncomfortable at his newfound position of leadership. Every few seconds, he removed his perfectly clean glasses to wipe them on his white pocket-handkerchief, scrubbing with grim determination at an invisible speck of dust.

Maryanne, dark circles under her eyes, stretched, yawning, in a seat several places away, while Steve fidgeted, his eyes downcast.

An air of tension pervaded the room, threatening to strangle all within. The council could feel it, in their bones, in their blood, the scent of ozone that accompanies a gathering tempest.

Windows, set into the wall at intervals of a few feet, provided little light in the cold, shadowy noon. Lashes of rain whipped against the glass as thunder rumbled outside.

Next to Sawyer, a raven-haired woman about his age, her mouth set in a strict line, muttered under her breath:

"Where are *they?"*

Sawyer raised a calming hand.

"They're coming. We must be patient, Ludmilla. You know as well as I do what they are about to undertake."

The congregation fell into a few minute's silence, broken only by the creak of the door opening.

Elizabeth and Preston stood in the threshold. At Sawyer's gesture, they took their place at the podium.

"Have you made your decision?" asked the man sitting on Sawyer's left.

"We have. We will find the Devil, and we will kill him or die trying," Elizabeth replied, with only a faint note of hesitation in her voice.

"Very well. You are brave, children, to carry this burden," Sawyer said sadly, "The rest of the Gateway shall do its part to aid in your mission, but ultimately, it's up to the two of you."

"We know," said Preston this time, "and we accept the risk. If there is a way to somehow put a hole in the Devil's defenses, we will do anything we can to make it happen."

"You may be seated," said Sawyer.

They did so, sliding into the two remaining seats, completing the gathering.

"Now, we must discuss our plan of attack," he said.

"A small party will journey through the tunnels to the Lobby, yourselves included. He'll be prepared; of that I have no doubt. We'll do anything we can to flood him out, as he is strongest when within his own domain. Once he's outside, our forces will hold the Angels, and whatever else he has in store for us, off long enough for you to incapacitate him. Once we have him secured upon the altar, before he can regenerate, you will end this, once and for all. And so the Devil falls," he said.

"And so the Devil falls," echoed the table.

As if in response, the vow was followed by a crack of lightning from outside, illuminating the room for an expansive instant in ghastly light, throwing everything into sharp relief.

"Doesn't it all seem too... simple?" Elizabeth asked, breaking the hypnosis. "I mean, the Devil won't just be sitting in the Lobby, waiting to be killed. I know him better than any sane person could wish. He always has some trick up his sleeve, some horror just waiting to be unleashed," she stated. Preston's hand met hers under the table, giving it a reassuring squeeze.

Sawyer replied, "We are prepared for such an eventuality, but we must make haste if we are to strike before he catches wind of our operations. The council is adjourned."

As the members of the Gateway rose to their feet, Preston met Elizabeth's eye. Wordlessly, a resolution passed between them: they would die together to end the monster that had ruled their lives for so long.

CHAPTER 36

"Are you sure about this?" Maryanne asks.

We sit down on a large pair of luxurious couches. We nod simultaneously, we discussed it so long that there was not a shred of doubt in our minds anymore. The feeling that this could be a final goodbye not just to Maryanne but also the Gateway clouded my mind. It wasn't the most enjoyable thought to have before going to fight the Devil to the death and it certainly did not help with my confidence.

"You can do it", says Maryanne.

This belief coming from Maryanne was rare. She would normally be more skeptical, perhaps trying to talk us out of this but she seemed to have caught on that there was no changing our minds no matter what persuasive tactics she were to try.

"I know we can," responds Elizabeth, she is coldly confident about this situation. "If we can find the Devil without being killed then I know we will kill him," she said.

I certainly don't have the same trust in myself but if she believes that we can do this then so do I. "Then this will be a goodbye but hopefully not forever," says Maryanne.

"Only for now," I tell her, coming across much more reassured than I truly am.

I stand and begin to pace a circle written in my mind across the dark floor before us. My back is facing Maryanne and Elizabeth somewhat intentionally as I want to give them an individual goodbye while still keeping an eye on Elizabeth, she seemed a little on edge, like she was hiding something. If she was, she was doing it well. With my back still turned I heard a small thud and gasp but who made the noise is impossible to say. I turn around to see Maryanne with a dagger aflame clasped tightly in her hand and Elizabeth unconscious bleeding out onto the floor beside her.

Without a second thought I charge at Maryanne grabbing her by the shoulders and tackling her to the ground beside Elizabeth. I see her dagger slowly slip from her hand and hit the floor with an indescribable power, the impenetrable marble of the Gateway laying cracked and destroyed. We both begin to lunge for the dagger but the cracks in the rocks are spreading apart and I fall between two large cracks and begin to dangle over the endless black abyss sitting below me.

Maryanne grabs the dagger as I slowly try to pull myself back over the ledge and as I do Maryanne stands over me ready to deliver the final blow. As she lowers the dagger towards my head she suddenly gasps and drops the dagger, her hand howling with pain. I seize her momentary loss of focus and pull myself up over the ledge and grab the dagger and stick it into Maryanne's back with as much force as I can muster. The shock of having delivered the life ending swing to another human's life does not even enter my mind as I quickly rush over to Elizabeth. She still has a pulse but it seems as if her skin is graying. I try to pick her up but my arms are much too tired to carry her and I sit on the floor accepting defeat.

As I lower my head I look over to see what should be Maryanne's lifeless body but instead I see the body of Steve. What had been Maryanne's face just moments before was slowly transforming into the recognizable face of Steve. My heart skips a beat as I stand to go examine Steve's lifeless body, but instead see a slow trickle of blood making a river through the floor coming from the closet where Maryanne had been just seconds before leaving to say goodbye to us.

CHAPTER 37

They rushed into the room, leaving Steve dead on the cold hard floor. In the room lay Maryanne, everything about her drenched in her deep red blood. Elizabeth gasped at the sight, and Preston closed his eyes and everything went dark for him. Regaining his senses, he rushed over to Maryanne who was staring blankly at the bright white ceiling.

"No one should have to die this way Preston," Elizabeth said, tears lining her voice and eyes. Preston nodded.

"It was most likely that dirty rat Steve. He must have been worried that Maryanne would snitch on him," she said.

It was obvious she had been stabbed multiple times, and beaten. She had a black eye, and in parts of her chest you could see her rib cage and a slash going down her lung. Gasping for breaths, but only succeeding in inhaling large amounts of blood, Maryanne used all of her energy to turn her head towards Preston. It was then that a new wound was revealed, a six inch gash running along her neck spewing an amount of blood neither of them could ever imagine was possible to be in the body.

Maryanne tried to smile, but ended up coughing, spraying Jackson Pollock-like designs on Preston's face. He did not wipe them up though, as he was too heartbroken to be with the young optimistic Maryanne as she bled to death. In between ragged, and unsuccessful breaths, she managed to get out the words,

"Preston. *Elizabeth.* Tell me a story," she turned her head back to the ceiling, and Preston and Elizabeth exchanged worried glances. Her time was almost over, and neither one of them knew any stories by heart. Desperate, Elizabeth started muttering, and then cleared her throat.

"Once there was a girl named Everleigh," Elizabeth started. "She was friends with everyone. Even the insects that crawl and the murids that scampered the earth."

"She was also friends with the birds, and the squirrels. The colorful butterflies, and the exotic caterpillars. Through all of the many friends that she had," Preston continued, "her most enjoyable moments was when she was alone watching the sunset on a cliff near her home. The yellow, orange, and purple all blended together to make the beauty that she enjoyed," Preston stopped, Maryanne's eyes were not moving around, as if she was Everleigh herself watching the sunset.

Her voice cracking with unimaginable grief, Elizabeth finished the story.

"One day, the sunset was so captivating, that Everleigh closed her eyes and drifted into the sunset. Upon her arrival, she was embraced with warmth, happiness, and *love,*" as if on a cue, Maryanne's eyes fogged over, and she went limp. Elizabeth burst into tears, while it took Preston a great deal of effort to prevent crying. Picking up Maryanne, he put her on the bed that was across the room, and gently closed her eyes. Elizabeth went into Preston's arms, full with feelings of frustration, annoyance, and grief.

"We should have killed Steve more brutally," she told him in between hiccups.

"No Elizabeth, we still have to be good people. It is bad enough that we must kill people anyway."

Elizabeth looked at him with eyes that were unmistakingly desperate.

"We have to win. Not only for us, Preston. For Maryanne. She didn't deserve to die. Everyone makes mistakes."

"I know," Preston said, letting a tear shed from his eye. "she just happened to endure the consequences."

"You know what Preston?" Elizabeth said, her voice sounding stronger.

"Yes?"

"I'm going to murder the Devil so *fricken'* bad, I might just be the devil myself," she said walking faster and ahead of him. Preston smiled, something he hadn't done in a while. He immediately stopped remembering what lay cold and still in the other room.

Licking his lips he said, "Trust me. We will. He will have more than a taste of his own medicine." With that, he caught up with Elizabeth, took her hand, and walked through the doors with overflowing determination.

CHAPTER 38

The crickets chirp as I make my way through the overgrown weeds. A hundred feet ahead of me is Elizabeth, moving swiftly through the brush. I can barely catch it when she makes a sudden left turn. I call her to slow down. When I finally catch up, I can see her looking back in the direction of the gateway.

"I never have stood up to the Devil," she said in a disappointed sigh. "I've been too scared to. I'm afraid he'll do something to us. We cannot mess up," she said. She continues walking through the darkness of the forest. An owl coos as we approach a clearing.

"Just saying, if this ends up a disaster, you can't blame this on me," I say jokingly, in hopes of lightening her spirits.

"If this ends up a disaster, I'll have no mouth to blame you," she says with a heavy laugh. "But if I did, I'd blame it on you anyway."

When we enter the clearing, I notice a blue square pinned onto the trunk of a tree.

"Is the entrance right under that square?" I ask Elizabeth.

"You mean that?" she said, pointing to the square that I was acknowledging. I nod a yes.

"No. That's there for stupid people who get lost in the woods. It tells them to go back. Because if they continue any further they'll be killed. But, no, the entrance is farther back in a pothole," she continues back into the forest, and immediately turns a sharp right.

"By the way, you better be really quiet," she says in a barely audible whisper. I continue to follow, until she comes to a sudden halt.

"Is this it?" I whisper, going to look at what she was crouching down at. It was a moss covered pothole.

"It is. Or it at least *was*, because I can't get this thing off," she says as she struggles to pull off the lid. I kneel down to help pull, but it feels bolted to the rim.

"Is it always this hard to take off?" I ask with a tired sigh.

"No, it is not this hard to take off usually," she responds obnoxiously.

"Ugh, they must've had some stupid hiker open it up which made them realize its too lose or something. But at the same time, this is the emergency entrance. So this isn't helpful," she throws a rock at it out of frustration, which causes the pothole to shatter into a bunch of pieces.

"How hard did you throw that?"

"Doesn't matter. Let's go," she says.

She pushes away the shattered pieces of the pothole, and starts climbing down the stairs. I look down into the darkness of the pothole, and take a deep breath.

Time to go see the devil.

CHAPTER 39

Preston and I were on our way to the Great Door. Everything here felt so familiar, the smell, the lighting, the way the cold hard floor felt. I knew that it would always be here, a place for beings associated with the Devil to mingle, and find their way, and yet, even being near the Lobby at this very moment, it felt so far away. A memory in my mind, my heart clawing through to try and grasp on to it one last time, because I knew. I knew and Preston knew, and most importantly our hearts knew that we would never see this place again. Who knows if we would ever see the grass, and the birds and the trees?

The Opening. The place where the once shy little Preston spied on me through the thicket. The place where every creature, the fox and the rabbit, the bird and the worm, the lion and the lamb, were at peace. It was a place that no longer would or could exist, and would be only a dream.

"Once we pass this door, *everything* we've ever known will be gone. No more sneaking out of class. No more looking out the window to watch the sunset. No more life.

Preston, once we walk through this door, we will never be the innocent little 14 year old school-kids that we could have been," I told Preston, who was walking like he had been here his entire life.

"Yeah." He replied. But the way he said it, I could tell he cared. Maybe it was that I led him down here, or he met the sweet young Maryanne here, but something about this place was special to Preston, but I couldn't, and wouldn't ask. We both stopped, having so much on our mind.

I stared at him, wondering how the sweet little boy, who was always looking at me, even since our early years at Coventry garden. How he turned 15 in a couple of weeks, and might not ever get to see his birthday. How someone so young would have to grow up so quickly. To have to understand that life wasn't all roses and rainbows until you were an adult. How you have to make sacrifices, and kill, and understand that even the most innocent of people would have to die, and sometimes you could never do anything about it. But what could he do? What could either one of us do? Our heads understood that this was the way life must be, but our hearts fought against it, knowing it would never win. This was life cut out for us. There was no running away from it. It would follow us like a shadow, killing everything and everyone that we cared even the slightest about. We had to charge headfirst, and understand that there was a possibility that we could die along the way.

"We should go," Preston started, knowing that thinking about how our life could end soon would never get us anywhere in terms of killing the Devil, "we can't waste time. Now, every moment is precious."

"Let's go," I replied.

We continued our way towards the Great Door asking every lucky charm that we ever heard of -even making a few up along the way- that we would make it through this. Other than that, all I could think about was Maryanne. It had been just moments ago when we had seen her take her last breath. She used to tell us things that could have gotten her in big trouble. Like that time when she told us that someone would become the Devil.

"Preston," I said, realizing my thoughts. It couldn't be, she couldn't be right.

"What?" he asked.

He stopped and turned around. He looked concerned. Although he was learning how to be tough, he was still a scared, little, stray kitten on the inside. I debated telling him about this, knowing that he was already going through so much, but at this rate, every piece of information mattered.

"Do you remember the time, in the Gateway, Maryanne was telling us that one of us might actually replace the Devil?" he looked shocked, and scratched his head.

"Um... yeah I do. Why?" he replied, trying to get what I was hinting at.

"Preston," I said, my voice getting unstable, "I think she was talking about you."

I expected him to be all surprised and taken back that I would think that. I *was* the Devil's apprentice, and knew all the ways I could possibly torture people. I might have the same chance that he did. But lately, Preston had become more blood thirsty. Not like a vampire, but he seemed way more determined to kill, and while before I could tease and joke around with him, now I'm afraid to get him mad. As kind as he is, he is the Devil's son, and one wrong move could change everything.

"Yeah. Yeah I know," he answered, looking away.

I guess another part of me expected him to realize this, because I seemed to understand his answer. I looked at him with concern, he knew that he would replace him but he never knew when, or how. There was a part of his future that was missing puzzle pieces that were critical. It could be the difference between life and death. Technically, he could become the Devil right after we kill the other one, or 60 years later.

"It's scary, you know? To know that after I kill the enemy, I become the enemy. I could *kill* you Elizabeth. You know that my Dad would do anything to kill things that do not please him. And obviously, one of those things is you!" Preston said, overwhelmed with emotions.

The poor thing was almost crying. My own lip was twitching, it was scary knowing that someone so close to your heart could end up being the reason for my demise.

"Look at me Preston. It's all going to be OK, alright? Even if you do end up doing something bad to me, I would never be mad at you. It's not your fault. This was the story we were writing, as unfortunate as it is, and we just have to play it out," I said, crying now. I was scared for Preston. The Devil had done so many horrible things.

"I guess," he said, wiping his tears, "whatever you do, don't try to save me Ok? I can't hurt you. If I start, you have to run. You can't try to find me, or console me. It won't work. Trust me. I know how this works," Preston added holding my shoulders square to his, and looking me straight in the eye.

"Except Preston, you don't. You and the Devil are and will always be different people. You both have a different life, and mind, and you don't know how that will play out for you. As for running away and hiding, I can't promise you that. I will never ever be able to promise you that. As much as you want to and hope that it would be true, I can't leave you. I will do everything in my power to make sure you're ok," I looked at him, alternating between his eyes.

We had gone through so much together, and I wasn't about to leave him for my own safety. He rolled his eyes, and walked away leaving me alone in the hallway.

"You're really stubborn, you know. I ask you to do *one thing* for me, and you just can't," he said. He took me by the hand and led me towards the door. He knew, and I knew. I wasn't going to change my mind. He was like a brother to me, and siblings don't leave each other.

We were walking faster now. He seemed really annoyed and the air was tense, so no one talked. We reached the Great Door in no time. We looked it down. It was big, tall, and intimidating. The Lobby was on the other side. From here on out, our lives would change forever.

Giving me a mini heart attack, someone opened the door. A head peeked out, grinning. The person opened the door wider, revealing a face that could not be mistaken for. It was John DeRusa.

"Elizabeth," he said with a grim look on his face. I looked away, it was hard to look at someone who I had killed, even if I had changed. The misery I had caused him and his family. No matter what I did, they would never forgive me.

"Hi, John," I said in a *please-let's-not-do-this-now* voice.

"Don't 'Hi, John' me. Puh-lease. I have been stuck in this hell circle for so long. I have literally given up all hope of heaven," he said, rolling his eyes.

"Come on John. You know he forced me to," I said as I pleaded for his understanding.

"Yeah right. You could have said no!" he answered angrily.

"He would have killed me!"

"So you killed me instead?" he snapped.

"You don't know how hard it was for me to do it! I liked you a lot!!"

"That's supposed to make me feel better?! 'Oh yeah, I liked you a lot, but I killed you. But I liked you a lot!' That's pathetic Elizabeth."

"You don't know what it's like," I argued, "You don't know what it's like to be controlled by someone who could take everything away from you!"

"Maybe I don't. But I do know the sickening feeling you get when you see your mother's face twisted and contorted with pain after seeing her son in a pool of blood on his own bed. You don't know the feeling of watching her pray to her son in heaven, when really he's in this hell pool."

"Well, at least they weren't fighting all the time! At least they care! If I died, my parents wouldn't care at all!" I said, trying to pull off this card.

"Oh don't give me that Liz! I know that you used a radio recording. Don't act like your parents were ever home. You fooled me. I let you. I paid the price. So stop acting innocent Elizabeth. You know exactly what happened," he said.

Before I could respond Preston pulled me aside.

"Arguing won't help Liz. I don't know what you did or what you didn't do and for what reason, but this will go on forever if you don't stop. You hurt him. It makes sense. You killed him. So just cave in," he said looking me straight in the eye. I looked away embarrassed.

"But-," I started but Preston cut me off.

"How do you not understand Liz? My Dad sent him. He wants something from us. If not, he would let us come. So go apologize, and see what's up," he said.

I snarled at him, and he cocked his head at me. It reminded me of a parent disciplining their kid. I guess I know who the kid is here.

"Do I need to say it twice, Elizabeth Gray?" he said gripping my arms harder.

I shook my head and he let me go, nodding his head towards John. I went over.

"Want to argue some more, Elizabeth? Or do I need to talk about how you wrote that note?" he asked.

He was trying to press me. Part of me wanted to respond. Another part wanted to punch him. A third part was going to listen to Preston. I decided on the third.

"I'm sorry John. I can't say anything about it. I killed you," I said.

He looked unsatisfied, and definitely did not forgive me, but he could tell it was an improvement, so he stopped.

"Come on. He wants you," he said, rolling his eyes.

He stopped to guard the door, and I walked through, Preston following close behind.

"What are you doing?" John asked him like Preston was cuddling with a pig.

"Going with her excuse you," Preston said, offended.

John turned to me. "Tell your knight in shining armor to leave. "He only wants you."

"Elizabeth, don't go! You know what he'll do! I can't let you go!"

Preston was in his panic mode. I smiled at him, adoring his care for me. But now was not the time. Besides, I knew how cruel the Devil was. If he planned to kill me, he would do it in front of Preston.

"Look Liz, it's either your boyfriend and you stay out here, or you come with me." John was getting annoyed. Besides, Preston just told me NOT to argue, so technically I was listening to him.

I paused. Bad things could happen. But without meaning to, I agreed. I looked back at Preston's face that was saying so much. Still, I walked through the door with John, awaiting the Devil.

I walked with John, and could hear Preston pounding on the door yelling my name over and over again. He was crying, my name getting shakier each time he said it. His pounding faded out as I got farther away from the Great Door.

All I could hope was that this wasn't the last time I would hear his voice.

CHAPTER 40

The Devil smiles as I walk into the Lobby.

"I knew you couldn't refuse another chat with me," he says laughing.

I don't respond. I keep my eyes set on his. He begins to slowly pace a circle around me as he speaks, "You know, Elizabeth, I have been thinking over these past few days and I seem to have come to a realization," he paused letting the only sound now be what I would assume to be Preston fighting to enter, "I have come to realize that I am not the one who should be killed, Elizabeth. I am not the person responsible for all the terrors and horrors the world has seen. I see now that if I had been wise, if I had been wise I would have seen that it was you a long while ago, seen that you were a murderer without thought, a ruthless killer destined to become ruler of a dark and evil world. A killer with no boundary and no limit. If I were wise I would have killed you," he uttered the final few words of his speech with such anger that he was spitting with each word.

I laugh. There seems to be no other reasonable reaction to this. The Devil attempted to clear his name by saying that the cause for anything he had done was because of a teenage girl.

"Do you not remember the countless lives you have taken? Do you not know the pain you have ensued?" he shouts at me.

"I'll kill you. I have murderer, yes. But I have never murdered with joy or passion as you do. Today that changes, Devil. Today I will kill you, I will kill you and I will enjoy it," I threaten.

Though for a second he seems intrigued by my statement the Devil quickly rebounds to an evil smile.

"If you choose violence for your death, then violence you shall get," he says pulling his long shining blade from his inside pocket.

I charge for him. My goal at first was to grab the blade from him and then plunge it to his chest but the Devil seems to be taking this fight unusually seriously. He is not laughing or enjoying himself. He is charging for me, hurling chairs and tables as near to my head as possible. As I charge I see my mistake. If I don't manage to take the blade from the devil I will have nowhere to escape. He has set a blockade surrounding the area where I would have escaped from before. I lunge for him and grasp the glistening blade in my hands for a heartbeat and then fall to the floor.

As blood drips from where my hand was sliced by the blade the Devil stands from his kneeling position. He stands slowly turning the blade in his hands.

"Goodbye Elizabeth," he says quietly and raises the dagger above his head. As he pulls his arms down ready to penetrate my skin, the door behind us opens.

CHAPTER 41

The Devil's face showed shock and surprise. I pushed my dagger against the Devil's harder, trying to get it out of his hand. I had the upper hand, the element of surprise. He had not seen me coming, he was expecting Elizabeth to be the one he was against. But he regained his posture quickly and fought back.

"Hello Preston," he said to me with a devilish smirk on his face.

"Hello father," I replied to him, in an equally accursed face.

I pressed his blade away with all my force and managed to push him back. I took a step back and the Devil took a step forward lunging at me with his blade in the air. He brought it down and I stepped out of the way quickly, slashing my knife to his side but barely managed to touch him. I left only a small tear in his suit. I stepped back once more, and the Devil seemed to retreat a bit.

"What's wrong?" I asked him, "Losing your touch?" I said with a hint of mockery in my voice.

"If you kill me, Preston, my son. You know you will replace me... as the new Devil," He said to me.

I looked deep into his eyes, looking for false information. But there was no point. He was most likely telling the truth. I didn't want to believe it, I didn't want him to know I did. So instead I argued.

"Not true, Maryanne found a book on how to defeat the Devil and it said that we needed to destroy their most prized possession."

"Ah yes, I suppose she would eventually inform the Gateway about that," He replied nonchalantly.

"What do you mean eventually? You knew that she knew that she could kill you," I asked him.

"Well yes, I'm the Devil, I know who goes into the restricted section and what they take out of it." He said.

I realised my question had, in fact, been a stupid and obvious one to ask.

"How do you know?" I asked him.

"I placed magic on the books, that one especially," He admitted to me. "so I knew it had been taken out, but what I didn't know was by who. So I kept a sharp eye out and realized that everytime I watched over her training or when I entered a room she was in, she coiled back just a little. She would look at me with questioning eyes, like she was trying to figure something out. So I had my theory, I just needed to confirm it. So I sent both Maryanne and Elizabeth on an assignment. I found the book in their room. I looked over it again, I wanted to know every single detail about what could bring me down. I read everything she had. But one thing. On the edges of the page, in a print so small it took the biggest magnifying lens to see it. 'The eldest offspring of the Devil is to take his place if killed in a mortal way.' " He recited to me. So he knew. He knew everything all along.

"So you knew that you needed me," I told him.

"Yes. I had the chance to first meet you when you were little. Only I hadn't known you were vital to me. You met Elizabeth that day too. And you two got along well so when I needed someone at Coventry Garden years later, she was the perfect choice."

"It was all a setup," I whispered.

"Indeed Preston, and you should know that being the Devil is not an easy thing to be. So I'll spare you, my son," He said.

He raised his dagger over his head. I knew what was coming.

"This is mercy Preston, the world is better off without you on the dark throne. You would die on your first day, so I'll just speed the process up for you," He said.

The blade hit a spot of sunlight before it came down on me. And I heard the sound of flesh being stabbed, yet felt no pain.

I opened my eyes.

Elizabeth.

She stood in front of me. She had gotten there faster than light. So fast I had not heard her running. She turned around to face me. Gasping for air, eyes losing their light with every passing moment. She crumbled like sand into my arms, and I laid her down on the carpet that was slowly becoming a dark burgundy color. The dagger was pressed deeply inside of her chest, through her ribs and directly into her heart. I was in too much shock to fully understand what had just happened. Not a tear could be shed. I just sat there, with her head on my knees, as I bent over to look at her. Her chest rose slowly and in painful ways. Her heartbeat, a memorized sound inside my mind, was slowing. Her time bomb on life was ticking it's last ticks. It would soon go off, she would soon be gone.

"No, Lizzie, stay with me. You're alright, you'll be back up again in a second," I said to her, trying to convince her, only I knew that deep down I was saying it to myself.

To convince myself. She looked at me, still trying to breathe as much as she could.

"Someone had to t-take it.," she said to me as best as she could, "I-i couldn't let it be you," she admitted.

Soft tears ran down her cold pink cheeks. They shimmered in the light and ran down her neck, slowly, agonizing me.

"Please don't go Lizzie, i can't-"

"Shhh, don't talk about me going. Don't say you can't go on," she breathed out shakily. When she inhaled she looked like she was suffering the worst pain imaginable.

"But I can't," I whispered back to her.

It was the truth. What was there left for me now? Coley was dead, Maryanne was dead, Elizabeth was dying. Everyone's death was my fault. I could do nothing to save them. I was cursed. Not because of the title I possessed, but by the blood on my hands. I didn't have to be named the son of the Devil. Even if nobody had known, even when nobody including myself had known, I was cursed. Living a half life where everything seemed to be going wrong. Like the universe had always planned on making me the most unfortunate person. To have the most unfortunate life. It was what it was. Sadly, I couldn't change that. But if I could I would. I would do anything to, because if I could and I did, people would still be alive and well. They would be with me now. Happy, lively, full of hope.

Elizabeth placed her hand on my cheek and smiled.

"I love you, Preston. Even when I had not admitted it to anyone or even myself, deep down in my soul I loved you. And I did a pretty crappy job at showing it to you. You deserve someone better than me. One that has no bad habits, no killing habits. One that can make you smile and never doubt her. Because you never doubted me. And people should be treated the way they treat others. And you treated me better than I ever did you," she whispered.

Those were the last words of Elizabeth Carter Grey. Love of my life. It killed me even more because I had doubted her once. And she would never know that I had not been completely honest all the time like she had thought. But I suppose having a clear conscience when you go along is the best way to. She could be at peace, knowing, no, thinking that I was better. That I was all good, even if i wasn't. That's how I would have liked going.

Her hand turned limp in mine, I looked at it as It did so and I furrowed my eyebrows. There on the palm of her hand was a grey spot. Where had I seen that color before? The Devil. The broken rings...when i broke them, the Devil weakened, some parts of him turned that colour too. I hurt Elizabeth. I let her hand go, this just added to the pain that was already afflicted on me.

This was the moment I knew I would never be ready for. I was young, I still had my whole life in front of me. But did I? Was I really alive if she was gone?

"No," I said.

I placed my hands on the side of her head firmly. Pushing the hair out of her face messily, bringing my face down to hers, I placed her forehead against mine.

"Don't go, don't go. You're not gone, you're not. No, no, no you just can't. Please," I begged down to her.

The tears finally came. They ran down my cheeks and on to hers, mixing with the ones that had been shed by her beautiful eyes. Her shirt and the carpet beneath us, was now completely stained a bright crimson. I looked up, my eyes were puffy and red from crying, and looked at the Devil.

"This is all your fault," I said to him in a calm and dark voice.

"No Preston, it's yours," he said.

At that moment, everything inside me felt different. I was hurting, everywhere. Unimaginable pain, worst that death. And I just snapped.

CHAPTER 42

Preston watched as the life faded from Elizabeth's rapidly graying eyes. The intricate hilt of the Devil's knife protruded from her chest as though it had grown there, a red stain spreading from the epicenter of the wound. Her breast rose and fell once faintly before stilling. A look of vague surprise still occupied her visage. Blood stained her parted lips.

Preston, on his knees beside her, shook her gently, receiving no reaction from her. Her pulse was faint in her wrist. He gripped her hand tightly as it began to cool.

"Elizabeth?"

A dam broke inside Preston, and the tears came, sliding down his face and mingling with the dark blood lying thickly on the tiles.

"Please, Liz, come back to me, you'll be alright, you *have* to be - ELIZABETH!"

Preston wept, lifting her onto his lap, holding her in his arms, cradling her protectively, his cries subsiding to indistinct gurgling.

From behind him, the sound of sharp footfalls reached his ears. The Devil.

"It didn't need to end this way, son. You know that. This is exactly what could have been avoided, had you stood by my side. It may have been her fate, but I have a way of getting around such trivialities."

Unresponsive, Preston put his head down, in a fetal position, Elizabeth's head on his lap.

"Please, Preston, don't make yourself the next unfortunate casualty. I would hate for this night to end with any more blood on my hands."

Preston's tear ducts had emptied, and yet he sobbed on.

"This is your last chance, boy."

Finally, Preston turned, and what he saw infuriated him. The Devil stood above him, impossibly tall now, stretching nearly to the ceiling. His hand, smooth and pale like a drowned man's, was outstretched. His eyes burned entreatingly.

Shaking, Preston rose to his feet, letting Elizabeth's limp form fall to the ground. Though his body trembled, his expression was steady. His eyes shone, mirroring those of his father, and there was something new in them, shining out of them. They spoke of murder. They spoke of hate, and for the first time in centuries, the Devil was truly afraid.

"You killed her. You actually *killed* her. She saved me, took my place, and now she's dead. Because of you."

"Preston..." The Devil took a step back, regained his ground.

"Now I'm going to kill you, father."

And Preston felt that it was true; he was the son of the Devil. He knew it, then, with a crippling certainty: this was his father he was facing, his father who had killed Jonothan and Chalice and

(*Oh Elizabeth oh my love gone gone gone down in the Lobby where the stars don't shine*)

countless others, who's golden blood flowed through his own veins.

"I'm going to kill you. For real, this time. I can't make the sacrifices we've made worth it, I can't save those lost along the way, but I can at least have this."

The boy of old was gone from Preston's eyes. Gone was the child, the recluse, the lover; gone was the broken boy who had lost one friend too many. In its place was cold, unfiltered, alien deadliness. He took a step towards his father.

Elizabeth's knife in his hand alongside his own, he charged.

The Devil dodged, coming away snarling with a sleeve in tatters. Crackling viridian flames spread along the length of his brandished blade as though it were covered in oil. The room seemed larger than it had been initially; it had swollen to at least twice its original size, the roof stretching twelve, sixteen, twenty feet high...

Preston's second frenzied strike nearly slashed the Devil's neck before it was deftly parried.

Preston overbalanced, tripping and nearly falling, allowing his opponent to carve a deep channel across his ribcage. Blood gushed from the exposed, raw flesh, the tissue and tendons beneath like a cheap cut of red meat.

Flames flickered across his skin, searing it on contact. A mortal wound was barely avoided by a quick pivot. His two blades shining in the lamplight, he stabbed upwards. The Devil parried once more, his hair plastered to his face with perspiration.

Grinning madly, his face a stretched mask of agony, Preston fought his father, showers of sparks flying when their blades met. The room was definitely growing; it was closer to a vacant ballroom now than an office, with the desk looking ever more dwarfed by its surroundings. The walls began to glow from within, bathing the room in a wash of red light.

With a roar Preston leaped, knives outstretched, one piercing the Devil's suit at the shoulder, drawing blood - red with just a hint of gold. His arm pinned the Devil's hand to his side, against the wall, before Preston received a fist to the stomach and went skidding, his head hitting the desk with a *crack* and sending papers flying in every direction as the lamp toppled over and shattered on the floor. He had barely risen when the Devil was upon him, fists flying, stabbing and slashing at anything he could find. The sharp teeth within his open mouth flashed dangerously as Preston struggled to get up beneath him.

"You should have learned by now, boy: no one escapes me, in the end!"

Preston could hardly do more than groan faintly as the Devil held his knife above him, the hand holding it covered in blood, some his own.

"I'll miss our games." The knife came down.

The crack of a bullet filled the space, its report echoing off the tiled floor and stone walls.

And the Devil was off him, screaming in pain, clutching his shoulder, as Sawyer, his ear streaming with blood, burst into the room, followed by a half dozen agents of the Gateway. Each held a knife, and a smoking gun was gripped tightly in Sawyer's left hand. The Devil sneered.

"Of all the soldiers of the Gateway! They chose *you*, Sawyer, to replace the late and great Challice? Oh, what dark times we've all fallen on, my old friend. And to think that you really believed you could kill me."

As Sawyer raised his gun in disgust to fire at his enemy, the Devil threw his head back.

Dropping his weapons, the leader of the Gateway screamed the command:

"Cover your ears!"

A piercing whistle echoed from deep within Devil's throat, high and chilling, an alien screech-owl's aria that grew expeditiously to a fevered volume.

From beneath the tiles came a low moan. The ground shook as it crumbled and cracked, expanding fissures spreading from the Devil out across the warped room.

By his feet, a hand burst from the ground, smooth and white and nailess. For a moment, it grasped blindly around, seeking purchase. Then the rest of the thing emerged in an explosion of ancient dust.

It had certainly once been human. Dull blank eyes stared from lidless sockets in a round face, fixed on a point in space far in front of it. It was not much taller than five feet, gangly and thin, dressed in a torn yellowed dress-shirt and jeans that may once have been blue. A fish had eaten away a good portion of one bare foot, and a few toes were missing from the other. Algae and plants covered its skin thickly in some places, giving it an overall green-tinted appearance. Water-growing weeds covered its long-haired head like a bizarre wig, and its mouth was a black cave. Its neck was slit, the wound long since washed of blood. A fish had laid eggs that had never hatched in the distorted cage of his ribs. The corpse of Arthur Canden shambled forward a few feet, leaving damp partial foot-prints in his wake, and collapsed as it struggled to remaster the process of walking.

All around the Devil, the dead crawled their way from the earth, some fresh and almost whole, some little more than bare skeletons.

As the Devil's song ended, Sawyer's pursuers materialized from the shadows of the hallway behind him: several Angels, slightly injured by their previous fight.

The Devil raised one hand, the Coventry crest shining in the light, his wounded arm held stiffly at his side. He wheezed slightly as he spoke:

"Kill - Them - *All!*"

Some of the dead surrounded their lord while the rest surged forward, and the Battle of the Lobby began.

From the hallway came the sounds of combat as dueling members of the two factions came through the open doors, only then realizing what chaos they had walked into. The massive room, featureless but larger than any sports stadium, was filled with the din of steel clashing against steel - and flesh. The dead tore their former allies limb from limb even as their own old flesh decayed, those who were once united in purpose separated by the impenetrable veil of rot and dirt and maggots. Sawyer fought two Angels at once, twirling and ducking in a blur of cold steel. In the center of the tumult stood the wounded Devil, laughing at his enemies' vain attempts to reach him.

Something grabbed Preston's ankle.

He looked down and saw the grinning face of Alma Chalice.

She was very pale, almost bloodless, her cloudy eyes bugging out of sockets filled with dripping yellow pus. Badly broken spectacles sat on her long thin nose. Her neck was bruised and covered in a multitude of small cuts, her head lolling limply to the side. One of the fingers on her left hand, the one gripping Preston, was slightly sunken in a ring-shaped area of pink depression.

Her cold hand tightened like a vise as Preston struggled to free himself from her grasp. She spoke in a croaking whisper, a dark shadow of her former voice.

"Oh Preston, how very irresponsible you've been," she scolded him. "letting me be killed and all. I have half a mind to have you expelled!"

A weight settled in the pit of his stomach.

"Professor Chalice, I didn't mean-"

"Now, now, just accept it. You went off to chat with *Elizabeth*," her smile stretched impossibly at the pain the name caused him, "and left me to fight on my own."

The pus began to run steadily in a mockery of tears.

"Prof - It's not you, you're not right, he's controlling you, you're a trick, you're not real..."

"Are you so sure? The consequences of a broken contract, like my poor dear Arthur, are not the only ones who end up down here."

"Let - let me go."

"Why, but I have so much to tell you! Do you want to know what I saw before my neck snapped like a twig? What was shining in the depths of that toothy throat?" she asked and gave a little giggle. "I saw through, saw what was *real*, all the projections cast aside. I saw the thing under the earth, the thing that has been there forever and ever and ever, in the heat and the starless burning *light...*"

Preston kicked with free foot, the boot smashing into Not-Chalice's skull. Thin fissures spread from the point of contract. She was pulling herself up, oblivious to the damage, smiling putridly all the while.

"I'll show you! Just come with me! How you'll sing and dance and smolder in the flames!"

He flailed out, stumbled back, tripped, fell, landing hard.

Chalice's face was inches from his, yellow, broken teeth locked together. Rotten breath drifted between them.

"I'm sorry, Professor. We needed the rings we needed to kill him I shouldn't have-"

"BURN WITH ME!"

Her eyes widened as Preston's knife buried itself in her chest, the tip emerging out the other side.

"I'm sorry."

She keeled over, the Devil's hold slackening, as the boy struggled to his feet. For a moment, Preston stared at her limp form on the ground, bending down to gently close her eyelids, the milky spheres disappearing from view.

From behind came the call:

"Preston! The Devil!"

Sawyer stood among a pile of bodies, struggling to get past the Angels that were blocking the Devil's retreat. All around him, the tide had begun to turn, the dead once more losing their hold on the living world, Angels falling beneath the blades of their foes. The maw of the earth yawned in great gaping sinkholes; broken bodies fell over their expanding precipices.

Preston ran, arms pumping, unseen things cracking and crumbling beneath his feet. As Preston approached the ring around his enemy, the Devil turned, claws sliding out, spindly extra arms erupting through his skin and jacket as he began to transform. A slim girl with pale skin and short black hair dyed a bright pink at the ends, the only signs of injury the cut across her ribs and a bruised eyelid, stood by his side.

A silver streak appeared on Preston's left, hurtling towards him: Sawyer's pistol. He snatched it out of the air and fired.

A dark shape moved in front of the Devil, arms extended protectively. A girl, not much older than fourteen. The bullet buried itself in her skull and she collapsed, stone dead.

Pushing the corpse aside with the tip of his shoe, the Devil drew his own gun from his coat-pocket.

His first two shots missed Preston by a fraction of an inch. As he advanced, so did Preston, and the distance between them began to close. The clamor of the battle raging around them faded into a low hum as Preston was hit in the ear by a bullet intended for his face, their sole focus the other.

Preston cried out in agony, dropping the pistol, and the Devil leveled his own with the boy's forehead.

And then he was off balance, Sawyer holding him in a choke-hold from behind, forcing him steadily down. The Devil gasped for breath as it was squeezed out of him. At least five bare white arms were pinned to his sides along with his two sleeved ones.

He cocked his head to the side, as if in puzzlement. And then, slowly, pityingly, he smiled.

"You always were a slow learner."

Preston lunged for the fallen gun an instant before it happened. The Devil's head, like some monstrous owl's, turned a full 180 degrees, ending facing Sawyer. The skin of his skull stretched as his jaw unhinged like a serpent. Row after row of glistening fangs jutted from his mouth, too many for his human face to accommodate, carving his full red lips into wet chunks which crept down his torn dress shirt like slugs, leaving a trail of blood behind them. Sawyer, his face a mask of shock, didn't have time to scream before his face was bitten like a savory chunk of meat.

Moaning horribly, he fell to the ground, clutching a face that bled in more places than he could count, an eyelid sliced along the center oozing and translucent whitish jelly, his hands doing little to staunch the inexorable flow of blood from his veins. Releasing the Devil, he collapsed in a twitching heap.

The Devil paid little heed to the man, turning instead to Preston.

His face was little more than a mouth and a pair of white burning eyes, his many hands bony claws, their fingers connected by webs of stretched skin. With a sound of warping, twisting bones, his spine elongated, tearing his shirt to expose his ribcage, its pointed ends breaking through his skin. He spoke in a gurgling roar, like water pouring down a gutter after a storm, that was not just heard but *felt*.

"KIIIILLL... YOU."

Preston snatched the gun off the cold floor. As his finger closed around the trigger, a piercing pain shot through his arm as it came away from his shoulder. The Devil, eight feet of pure murder, dangled him in the air by disjointed limb. Another arm came from behind the Devil's head, fingers flexing and scrabbling, nails like small daggers poised to strike.

"YOU ARE GONE, LITTLE BOY, DEAD AS CAN BE. ENJOY THE LIGHT. ENJOY THE VIEW. ENJOY MY LOBBY."

Millions of voices babbled and buzzed within his head like a hive of some unimaginable insects.

Light forever in my Lobby life ETERNAL dead dead deegggggghhhhhh

All at once, the voices of the Devil began to scream as endless arms groped weakly for the hilt of Elizabeth's knife, which had sunken into his chest, a few inches below his heart. As his hot blood flowed over Preston's fingers, the boy was plunged, against his will, into his enemy's mind.

* * *

Massive pine trees rose from the damp ground, their needles littering the forest floor. The sound of running water permeated the cool, dry evening shadows.

The forest was silent, as if in anticipation of something beyond Preston's sight.

From far away, the sound of something large coming reached Preston's ears, crashing through the low shrubs. He dashed wildly to the side as an enormous ratite the size of a man burst into the clearing, thick beak snapping at the air, lidless eyes rolling crazily, paying no heed to the boy standing just a few feet from it. Its talons made deep indentations in the soft earth.

And it was gone, disappearing into the bushes on the far side of the clearing.

Seconds later, it was followed by a similarly agitated horse, not much larger than a small dog, with black stripes running along its length. Rodents scampered in its wake and birds flew above in a bizzare parade.

Preston waited, not heeding the warning of the rebelling forest, his knees locked together. The sharp, battery-acid smell of a storm filled the air, though the sky was clear.

Wait, not entirely clear. There was a faint white dot far above, getting larger, *hurtling towards him*.

It grew steadily, and as it did, so did the scent of electricity. He could just make out two interlocked rings, spinning and whirring, melting and congealing. The strength returned to Preston's knees and he was off through the trees, the ground humming beneath his feet, as though an earthquake were about to tear through the forest. A deadly light filled his peripheral vision.

As the thing crashed through the treeline far behind him, Preston flung himself on the ground, his eyes shut against the fiery light. The steady hum had become a roar. The eardrum within the ear to the earth burst and hot blood bubbled out.

An explosion shook the forest, a sonic boom like a thousand claps of thunder. Gradually, the roar subsided, muted by his injured ear, though every few seconds a loud popping could be heard. Opening his eyes just a sliver, he found that he was at the edge of a great crater. Fallen trees had embedded themselves in the soil, and chips of their bark had flown like daggers into their comrades and the few animals foolish enough to remain within a hundred meters of the crash. A large furry rodent lay dead, impaled by a sharp piece of wood, its blank shiny eyes staring at the obscured sky.

Black smoke covered everything, thick and venomous, slithering in sinuous coils from the invisible center of the crater, from which emanated a cold shine, like moonlight.

No smoke without fire.

The smell of burning wood hit Preston's nostril just as the source of the popping sound became clear: the forest was aflame. A tree nearby split along its trunk and burst, hot sparks raining down in a storm of fire.

Preston, the smoke filling his lungs, ran, but not before the light began to grow brighter, getting closer, probing, seeking, inquisitive. Dry coughs accompanied his hard, pained breathing. He staggered, bracing himself against a tree, only to realize that he was clutching little more than raging ashes. He quickly withdrew his hand to find his palm shiny, red, and raw.

He broke through the edge of the clearing, and in the distance he saw a shimmer and even through the haze of heat he knew that it was a river, bubbling along obliviously.

If I can just make it to the water...

A tree crashed to the ground behind him, and he tripped and fell, crawling on his hands and knees. The poison in his lungs filled his head, clouding his thoughts. Frenzied, like the animals he had encountered earlier, he made one last desperate lunge.

His burnt fingers touched the blissfully cool water. He collapsed as the screaming sky burst into flame.

* * *

Flames covered everything. Preston was on fire, but felt no pain; in fact, everything else felt quite distant.

He was under the earth, under everything, in an underground chamber below the crater. The sound of whirring and buzzing permeated the ghostly light. No sky was visible through the black hole in the ceiling.

Something stirred in the center of the chamber, near the floor. It rose, hovering, floating weightlessly until it rested midway through the air. Massive rings of some strange silver metal flashed through the air, almost fluid, molten. Flickering gaseous faces unlike any earthly creature's peered through the smoke, mouths gaping.

Amid the flames and the shadows, a white-hot eye opened, and spoke in a grating, somehow identifiable tongue.

Home.

* * *

The Devil was screaming with every fiber of his being.

Get it out get it out stop it stop it stopstopoutithurts

Preston fell from his grasp, straight into the sinkhole that had opened beneath him.

He hit stone, hard and unforgiving, and the first thing Preston registered was the pain, ripping through his limp arm, flooding his vision, turning it red.

Holes opened across the battleground, through which fell combatants, Gateway and Lobby alike.

Something hit the ground beside him, hard. Elizabeth.

The tunnel ceiling caved in behind her, blocking out the light, and they were alone in the tunnels of the Lobby.

A faint *whump-THUMP* sounded through the passage: a heartbeat. Every few seconds it was repeated, the ground reverberating along with its pulse.

His throat still stinging with the toxic smoke of long ago, hardly thinking, Preston bent down and, picking up

Elizbeth's body, slung it over his shoulder like a heavy, limp sack.

The tunnel ahead wavered and whispered, and Preston began to walk.

* * *

He didn't stop for what felt like hours. All around him was silent dark, solid and impermeable. Elizabeth's corpse seemed to grow heavier as the incessant drumbeat of the Devil's heart rose and fell like the tide, as the steady *plink* of some foul liquid landing in puddles on the floor faded to white noise, as Preston passed intersection after intersection, always sure of his choice, drawn by some irresistible magnetic force.

Occasionally, drifting from these diverging paths, came the sounds of small skirmishes, to which Preston paid little heed. Only when some sign of pursuit caught his ears did he hasten his stride, though the weight on his shoulder prevented him from sustaining such a pace for long.

The ground began to slope steadily upwards as he walked, the heartbeat fading the farther away he got from the core of the Lobby. His ears popped as the pressure released.

Suddenly, blindingly, a small rectangle of white light appeared far ahead.

As his eyes adjusted to the dark, he saw that he had arrived at the Gateway.

The stars above the white pillars of the great chamber were vibrating and spinning, out of control. The leaders of the Gateway grinned madly in their frames, their eyes absent from pitted oozing sockets. The meteorite had cracked along the center, cataracts spreading throughout the eye.

Gently setting Elizabeth on the ground, Preston walked directly to the altar, and sat down on the edge of the dais to wait.

He did not have to wait long. From the tunnel came a clattering and skittering like some massive centipede moving along the stone.

The thing that scampered into the room looked little like the man that it had a penchant to masquerade as.

The Devil's chest had opened like a vile mouth, from which spindly white arms protruded like a lizard's, carrying him aloft a few inches from the ground. His mask-like face, upside down, smiled at Preston blindly, its hair dragging along the ground. Blood dripped from the gash below his heat. Something was overlaid with his form, like a mirage, translucent and flickering: a fiery eye raged, shattered fragments of rings circling around it.

Rising, Preston regarded the thing calmly, and began to walk towards it.

"Hello, father."

The Devil launched himself across the room, leg-arms moving in waves like the oars of a galley. In the center of the room, they met, and regarded each other for a moment. Preston held a knife in his right hand, his other arm dangling uselessly at his side. As the Devil's claws slid out, the eye screamed.

Lunging and slashing, Preston led the Devil in a deadly dance, slicing through arms in a tornado of steel. Where they fell on the ground, they continued to move, spidery hands making their blind way into walls or flipping over and dying there, twitching on their backs. The Devil's head snapped and foamed, the spittle writhing on the floor as if alive. Talons raked Preston's skin, scrawling bleeding calligraphy. The eye was almost solid now, the man growing immaterial.

They ascended the dais as one. Preston realized with a sickening feeling that he had backed himself up against the altar, its sharp lip pressing into his shoulder blades. The Devil reared up on three white arms, bearing down on his foe.

Their eyes locked, and once again Preston was falling, hurtling towards those obscene orbs.

* * *

Light. Light everywhere.

Preston was under the Lobby again. It had changed little in the seven million years that had passed since the time of his last vision; the only sign that he wasn't in only the hole in the ceiling had disappeared under by the loose earth that had packed in over the centuries.

* * *

Preston's knife sunk into the Devil's eye just as the Devil's claw found his throat and tore at it.

He looked down, unbelieving, the now-material Devil's bleeding eye inches from his two, getting a faceful of blood. He collapsed on the ground next to the altar.

The eye hovered, triumphant at last, even through its agony, as its human shadow spoke:

"I have won, boy. At long last I have won."

From Preston's broken throat came a low gurgle: "You're - dying. You won't - make it."

"I can find a new body, rebuild what I've lost. Your Gateway will never be able to stop me. They will be crushed."

"Too - late. I - am - your *prized possession*, fool. You - just - wouldn't admit it. The rings were - just a piece, just one of your heads to cut off. That last shield is gone." Preston raised his torso off the ground, his unbroken arm flashing out, and the knife flew through the air.

Realization came to the Devil's face as he fell backwards, the shadow solidifying, impaled by the silvery metal, onto the altar with a grim finality as the hovering eye crumbled into ashes that rained down the solid corpse.

Preston sank to the floor, his duty done, eyes half closed as his dying hand found Elizabeth's cold dead one. He saw the stars grow brighter in the ceiling high above. As the golden, crackling blood erupting from his ruptured artery mingled with that of his father, Preston died.

EPILOGUE PART I

January 3

The new year's snow falls, heavy with words unspoken. In the chaos of the past few days, I have hardly found time to sleep, let alone write, but I believe that this must be set down, while it remains fresh in my mind. Even as I sit here in Chalice's office, released from the ward but still under periodical care, like an intruder, not entirely sure that she is really gone, I feel as though I can still hear the pulse of that infernal heart, now silenced forever, or so I sincerely hope with every fiber of my being.

A week ago was the Battle of the Lobby. Though I did not witness its end, I will recount what I can.

It began in the tunnels from the Gateway to the Devil's lair, tunnels now sealed forever under a million tons of rock.

As our group traversed the labyrinth, we found that we had walked into a trap. He was ready for us. It must have been that traitor Steve who told him the plan. He sent things after us, Angels and... other things, creatures from his home, some inhuman brood of teeth and claws and spines. Robert went down, guts unzipped, and there was nothing I could do to save him.

We fought our way through, drawing attention away from Preston and Elizabeth. Breaching his inner sanctum, I thought we had a chance. Then the dead began to rise.

So many. I have lost so many friends over the years to that monster. I would give anything to see them again, just not like that, not rotted and dried and filled with all his hate and rage. They were all there, Reed and Marley and all the others, and I nearly died by the hands of my long-lost comrades.

That pain was sadly dwarfed next to being bit in the face by the Devil. God, the agony... a hundred needles piercing the sensitive skin, my eyes, my lips, nearly drowning in a puddle of my own vital fluids. I felt like I was dying, choking on his scintillating internal fire, which had seared itself into my mind.

I am ashamed to say that I grayed out a bit after that, and remember little until later, in the tunnels, where I woke screaming. I couldn't see anything, though even above ground I doubt that my freshly vivisected eye and my one mostly whole one would have been able to detect much more than vague brightness. Kate and Sean helped me to my feet and told me about the sinkholes. I asked if we had been followed. No, they said, we were alone. The last they had seen of the Devil was him being impaled on the end of Preston's knife. I, however, was certain of one thing, as his heart beat from the walls: he was still very much alive.

I limped along, supported on either side by the other two. Along the way, we learned that the Angels too had become shut in their own maze, which they knew far better than we might have feared. We must have taken a wrong turn somewhere, as the pressure was increasing with each step, only stopping when we reached a dead end. We were ambushed. Sean took a bullet to the head before he could say "we're trapped" , and Kate was wounded in our escape. Even then, we only made it out through some miracle: each of them dropped to the ground simultaneously, twitching and shaking as though they were having some kind of a seizure, bleeding eyes rolling back in their sockets. And something happened then, so subtly that at first I hardly noticed: the heartbeat stopped.

I had little time to figure out what this meant before I was hurrying as fast as my screaming, twisted legs could carry me, arm around Kate's shoulders as hers was around mine, ears alert for the sound of pursuit. None came.

We ended up before the door, that hideous amalgamation of stone and metal. It had somehow been blown partly off its hinges and hung loosely from the frame. Once across, we were greeted by a terrible sight: the mural was crumbling, chunks of it bursting on the floor. Blood was bubbling forth in a fountain from the bowl at its base.

Along the path to the right, I withdrew my hand from the wall as the stone melded seamlessly into a wide, slick sewer tunnel. The smell of ancient, damp earth was quickly replaced by the oily, warm scent of decay, like a whole crate of potatoes left to rot in the dark of an abandoned basement corner. Within a few minutes, thick, viscous liquid like diluted honey had begun to flow sluggishly past my ankles, the warm tide rising steadily until it reached to mid-shin. I heard large rats scurrying and squeaking along ledges and through grates, searching for scraps of food in the raw poison of the sewage. Something furry floated past, brushing the exposed skin under my torn pant-leg.

At long last we saw the light, shining in through an open manhole cover, and I had to squint through my one good eye for minutes after. Above ground, we made it to a known entrance to the Gateway before collapsing in a stinking, dripping pile before the alley doorway.

I woke in the Gateway's medical ward, the pain in my eye a high shrieking under the gauze of the painkillers in my system. Next to me, propped up against her pillow, an IV in her arm, was Kate, and beyond her were others, dozens of others, some nearly unrecognizable, torn and battered and broken. Kate turned to me, saw I was awake, and smiled.

"He's gone. We won, Sawyer."

It took me a few seconds to register what she had said. How could we have won, with so many lying here, their broken bodies mingling horridly with the antibacterial sharpness? And then it hit me: gone. The Devil was gone.

From the nurses I learned the following information: I had been out for five days. My bones were fractured in many places, my ribs cracked, my face scarred (I shuddered as I ran my hand over the channels that that monster had carved there), and I was blind, almost certainly forever, out of my left eye. They had thought I would die, had been almost certain of it, but I had apparently managed to cling to life while I lay there on the white sheets, fed through the tubes trailing from the large metal contraption by my bedside.

The battle had ended for all much as I experienced, in isolated skirmishes throughout the tunnels. We had lost dozens of agents, some to the Devil, some to the Lobby itself as its tendrils came crashing down on top of them. Many were still missing, including Preston; a search had been initiated of the rubble. A mass funeral will be held tomorrow by the pond for the fallen.

Angels haven't been seen for days; either they've gone into hiding, or their connection with the Devil broke them when he fell, and they still lurk in the ruined Lobby pathways, gibbering in the dark as they are picked off, one by one, by the creatures who live there. We will find them, if we can, and they will be tried for their crimes. We must remember, however, our friend Elizabeth, and the degree to which the Devil corrupted his minions, threatened them, twisting them into his ideal killers, swift and silent and utterly ruthless.

A corpse had been found on the altar beneath the Gateway, a dagger in its chest, smiling serenely through full red lips: the Devil's final host, some poor man who had gotten too close to the thing under the Lobby to the Otherverse. Blood stained the floor, far too much to have come from the Devil, like a herd of animals had been slaughtered in there; a trail of it led from the room in red (and GOLD) footprints.

The Lobby is sealed off from the outside world. Who knows what's become of its inner gates; who knows what remains.

Now, on to what is, for the purposes of the Gateway, the most pressing matter: the Devil is dead. I can feel it, know it for certain this time; the rings have been shattered, the eye pierced. But it begs the question: why was the bloody trail of ichor leading from *the room? Where are Preston and Elizabeth? She died in the Battle, but her body hasn't been recovered. Something in me feels that he wouldn't have left her easily. So what has become of the Devil's killer, as I am sure he is?*

I think I know the answer, and it's that our little plot worked, down to the last detail.

Preston the Devil, the Eternal, with the lifeforce of a dying star flowing through his veins, changing him - such power, such horror. I pity any resigned to such a fate.

Preston, where are you? And when I find you, what will be left of you?

* * *

There was no ground beneath him. That was the first thing he noticed.

Preston opened his eyes, and wished he hadn't.

He was floating in the center of a great black void, suspended in the air, nothing below or around him, no way to tell up from down, without any point of reference. He tried to move, and drifted a few feet before coming to a halt.

At the edge of the churning, wriggling darkness, stars were dying, moving, screaming silently at the dead universe.

This is the end. I am at THE END. FINIS. AND THEY ALL LIVED HAPPILY EVER AFTER.

Something was coming towards him, and he saw that what he had mistaken for a star was a living thing. Its gasses and fumes formed almost recognizable shapes before dissipating back into the haze, like a dream half-remembered. The thing had rings like a planet, though these were corroded and metallic, not icy, pockmarked by pits and craters the size of moons. Great ray-wings beat the air as it grew steadily larger, filling his vision, its surface covered in cataracts like some immense eye, through which pure, devastating light shone. It spoke directly to Preston's mind, its voice weary with the ages.

It is done. The burden is yours now, young one. Thank you.

Who are you?

I am so very old. The hunt is over. I can finally rest.

I don't understand.

He was the last.

Is the Devil gone?

It chuckled softly.

I suppose the title fits. Yes, it's dead.

Then...

I'm dying, Preston, and when I go, there will be none of us left. You will ensure that we will never truly be gone. Through you, we live on. Now go. And good luck.

As the void rushed past him, receding in a blur, the thing collapsed in a burst of deadly light, racing after him, rays reaching like fingertips.

And then it was all gone, and he found himself once again in the bowels of the Gateway.

* * *

EPILOGUE PART II

I sat outside the Lobby. I do this every once and a while nowadays. I liked to watch her as she ran around in the tall grass, picking wild flowers by the dozen. Bright pink, yellow and the color of soft blue and white. She had her mother's grace and beauty. For a child, only five years old, I saw great potential. She grew more and more like me. I guess it made sense, after all, she was my daughter.

We shared only little things in common. The color of our eyes, the smile that showed you were up to something. But she was very much Elizabeth's daughter. They had the same hair, the unnatural charm they made everyone notice her. Even at her age people were fascinated by her. She was lovely, really, but hints of darkness had shown a couple times. Nightmares that never left her as she woke up in the night, haunting her. The way she would talk to the deceased in the Lobby, how she lied with such ease it was frightening. For God sake she was only five! She had stolen a book, and lied about it. My most valuable book, it was. But nonetheless, she wasn't old enough to understand the darkness written in those pages, the ones that spoke truth in black ink. She was truly, at many moments, the daughter of a killer and the Devil. And everyone knows, some day, she has the greatest chance of all, to replace me.

"Annabelle, come here," I heard her mother call to her.

Elizabeth was sitting besides me, not fully alive, but she was. In the years we have had Annabelle, she has aged well. She looked older, but not too old. Mature, but not serious. Happy, but not crazy. She had the perfect balance of everything. Capable of being the Devil's wife, co-worker and a mother at the same time. And she excelled at them all. Annabelle came running our way, smiling happily as her hair flew behind her. She came up and ran into me, holding me tight before letting me go a second later. She held her bouquet of flowers up in my face.

"Daddy, look what I got for mommy," she babbled excitedly to me. I smelled them and then smiled at her.

"They're beautiful, just like her. And you," I said to her as I touched the end of her nose.

She giggled and then took a couple steps over to Liz. She handed them to her and Elizabeth smiled brightly. She took them and kissed Annabelle on the head, thanking her for the flowers. I watched them talk to each other. Not paying much attention to the words that they spoke, but more on the scene that they were creating. Only it was distured.

"Sir! Sir!" I heard someone calling from behind me.

I Pulled my eyes away from my girls and got up to face the voice that called out to me. A man wearing a gray vest and white button up shirt ran over to me. He carried in his left hand a glass clipboard. He gasped for air when he halted in front of me.

"What is it, Jenson? It better be important, you know better than to disturb me unless it is," I told him, I was annoyed and I'm sure he could tell.

"Well, sir, there has been a development with Mr and Mrs Miller's case," He told me. "and not the good kind."

"What is it?"

"Well the thing is that, well, they sent the agreement away, replaced it with a fake," I took a breath.

"Thank you Mr Jenson, When you get back to the Lobby, be sure to take my blade out. It needs to be polished before use," I requested.

He nodded before scurrying off back to where he came from.

It seemed that my clients have broken a deal, a deal with the Devil. And there is only one way that ends.

ABOUT THE AUTHORS

BENJAMIN SLEEPER read all of H.P Lovecraft before you completed the works of Dr. Seuss.

HUDSON SCHUNK will destroy you at tennis. He lives in Connecticut.

MATÉ BLIER rides bicycles in the rain, for days on end. He lives in New York.

OLIVIA ROMAIN can stay afloat for hours, whilst playing water polo, better than you. She lives in California.

VERONICA PARÉ speaks effortless French, bien sur. She lives in Canada.

Together, they are:

The Ridiculously Talented Crew.